"Do you know anything about barrettes?" Garrett asked.

"Barrettes and bangs are my specialty," Whitney replied. "You probably didn't notice, but my hair has a mind of its own. I'm always trying to make it behave."

They were standing close together now. "And does it behave?" he asked.

"My hair?"

"Uh-huh."

"Uh . . . rarely."

"And how about you, Whitney? Do you always behave?"

She couldn't breathe, or think, but she could feel something potent and out of control quickly spread through her body.

Whitney glanced up and found Garrett watching her through narrowed, probing eyes. Somehow she knew that every fiber in his body was aware of her every move, her every expression.

"I always behave," she finally managed to say.

A sudden spark flared to life in his eyes. "Well, we just might have to do something to change that."

Dear Reader,

Warning! Don't read April's terrific lineup of Silhouette Romance titles *unless* you're ready to catch spring fever!

The FABULOUS FATHERS series continues with Suzanne Carey's *Dad Galahad.* Ned Balfour, the story's hero, is all a modern knight should be—and *more.* Ned gallantly marries pregnant Jenny McClain to give her child a name. But he never expects the powerful emotions that come with being a father. *And* Jenny's husband.

Garrett Scott, the hero of *Who's That Baby?* by Kristin Morgan, is a father with a mysterious past. He's a man on the run, determined to protect his daughter. Then Garrett meets Whitney Arceneaux, a woman whose warmth and beauty tempt him to share his secret—and his heart.

Laurie Paige's popular ALL-AMERICAN SWEETHEARTS trilogy concludes this month with a passionate battle of wills in *Victoria's Conquest.* Jason Broderick fell in love with Victoria Broderick years ago—the day she married his late cousin. Now that Victoria is free and needs help, Jason will give her just about anything she wants. Anything *but* his love.

Rounding out the list, there's the sparkling, romantic mix-up of Patricia Ellis's *Sorry, Wrong Number* and Maris Soule's delightful and moving love story, *Lyon's Pride.* One of your favorite authors, Marie Ferrarella blends just the right touch of heartfelt emotion, warmth and humor in *The Right Man.*

In the coming months, look for more books by your favorite authors, including Diana Palmer, Elizabeth August, Phyllis Halldorson and many more.

Happy reading from all of us at Silhouette!

Anne Canadeo
Senior Editor

WHO'S THAT BABY?
Kristin Morgan

Silhouette
ROMANCE™
Published by Silhouette Books New York
America's Publisher of Contemporary Romance

To those wild and wonderful Pokeno girls:
Judy D., Keroma, Judy M., Glenda, Grace, Linda,
Ava, Betty, Ann, Janice and Bobby.
I love y'all.

SILHOUETTE BOOKS
300 E. 42nd St., New York, N.Y. 10017

WHO'S THAT BABY?

Copyright © 1993 by Barbara Lantier Veillon

ISBN: 0-373-08929-5

First Silhouette Books printing April 1993

All the characters in this book have no existence outside the
imagination of the author and have no relation whatsoever to
anyone bearing the same name or names. They are not even
distantly inspired by any individual known or unknown to the
author, and all incidents are pure invention.

®: Trademark used under license and registered in the United
States Patent and Trademark Office and in other countries.

Printed in the U.S.A.

Books by Kristin Morgan

Silhouette Romance

Love Child #787
First Comes Baby #845
Who's That Baby? #929

KRISTIN MORGAN

lives in Lafayette, Louisiana, the very heart of Acadiana, where the French language of her ancestors is still spoken fluently by her parents and grandparents. Happily married to her high school sweetheart, she has three children. She and her husband have traveled all over the South, as well as other areas of the United States and Mexico, and they both count themselves lucky that their favorite city, New Orleans, is only two hours away from Lafayette.

In addition to her writing, she enjoys cooking and preparing authentic Cajun foods for her family with recipes passed on to her through the generations. Her hobbies include reading—of course!—flower gardening and fishing. She loves walking in the rain, newborn babies, all kinds of music, chocolate desserts and love stories with happy endings. A true romantic at heart, she believes all things are possible with love.

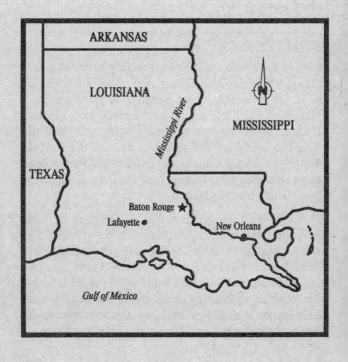

Chapter One

Whitney saw her new neighbor first, then the baby girl who was always with him. His daughter, Whitney thought as a bittersweet smile touched her lips. No doubt about it. In the bright May sunshine, their hair color was the same rich brown. The child looked so adorable. Tears sprang to Whitney's eyes, but she quickly blinked them away.

In more ways than she cared to admit, the little girl reminded her of Allison.

Swish... Whitney felt the ever-present ache in the center of her chest choose that moment to score another blow by slam-dunking its way to the pit of her stomach.

She drew in a deep, unsteady breath as a warm springtime breeze swept her shoulder-length auburn hair from her face. Would the pain of losing those she loved ever go away?

Once again the reminder that she no longer had her beautiful sister or her sister's child—though she'd lost them each in a different way—made her broken heart squeeze tight with emotion. Lisa was gone forever. And all common sense told Whitney that it was very likely she would never see Allison, her sister's little girl, ever again.

Oh, God, she could hardly endure that thought when it came.

It was all so unfair. To have a baby whom you loved so dearly taken away from you simply because you had no legal claim to her didn't make it right. Didn't love count for something?

Apparently not. At least, not where her brother-in-law had been concerned. After her sister's untimely death, Whitney had helped him care for her young niece, who had only been two months old when her sister was killed in a car crash. And he, like the manipulator she now knew him to be, had encouraged her, constantly saying to everyone how much he and Allison needed and depended on her. But after nearly three years of Whitney's caring for the two of them, her brother-in-law had suddenly packed up his and Allison's belongings and moved away from Baton Rouge without any warning and without so much as leaving behind a forwarding address so that Whitney could keep in touch with him for news of her niece.

She would never forgive him for that. Never. And while she had plenty of other good reasons to be angry with him, not knowing how her niece was, was the most painful. She couldn't help but wonder how much Allison had grown during the year since she'd seen her last, and if the strawberry blond, baby-fine hair she'd inherited from her beautiful mother was still the same color. And while many things in her life remained uncertain,

Whitney felt in her heart that she could never love another child as much as she loved her niece. Not ever.

She shoved her painful memories aside and again turned to watch as her new neighbor from across the street pushed his grocery cart away from the supermarket and toward his Jeep Cherokee truck, which was parked about seventy-five feet from her brand-new white Pontiac Grand AM.

In the past two weeks whenever Whitney had seen the man and child, they had been alone. Today was no different. At some given point she'd come to the conclusion that the man must be either widowed or divorced. But he kept pretty much to himself, and Whitney had a feeling that was the way he liked it. Which was just fine with her. Actually hunky-dory fine. It was too bad he had moved into her neighborhood, though—the man was in for a big surprise if he thought he went unnoticed. Nearly everyone on her street thought it their duty to know everyone else's business. In fact, her street probably had the best Neighborhood Watch program in all of Baton Rouge. Certainly the most attentive.

Her new neighbor didn't seem to notice her standing at the rear of her car, loading up her own bags of groceries in the trunk. Which didn't really surprise her at all. He hadn't seemed to notice her on the several other occasions when she'd tried to be neighborly and had waved at him from her front yard. But then, Whitney thought, why should he have? She was...well...she was just the kind of person who usually blended in with the scenery. Her bad-tempered father had once called her ordinary, and it was one of only two times in her life that Whitney had known him to speak the total truth. The other time had been when he'd told her sister, Lisa, that she was the pretty one in the family.

But the man she was looking at wasn't someone her father could have called ordinary. Not by a long shot. His broad shoulders, lean hips and powerful-looking arms, as well as his sun-streaked brown hair and tanned complexion, gave him the look of an athlete. And the quick, easy smiles he gave to his daughter...well, they could be classified as a ten on anyone's Richter scale.

Not that she was measuring, she quickly reminded herself. And not that she thought he—or his little girl, for that matter—looked extraspecial in any way.

Suddenly Whitney realized where her thoughts had taken her and she jerked her eyes from her new neighbor. Having a will of its own, however, her gaze fell upon the little girl seated in the cart. Whitney's heart did a slow backward somersault. The child was precious. Absolutely precious. So young and innocent—and apparently without a mother. So much like Allison. Again the raw, ever-present ache inside her felt as though it had been rubbed over with a rough grade of sandpaper.

But whether or not this child had a mother wasn't any of her concern. Not in the least.

Thank God.

Slamming the trunk closed, she walked around the side of her car and unlocked the door. In fact, she told herself grimly, if she had any sense at all, she'd completely ignore both the child and her father.

Though, heaven help her, no one knew better than she did that common sense wasn't always her strong point. At least not when a small, motherless child was involved. But she had made herself a promise and she planned on keeping it. If she continued to feel this ridiculous, overpowering need to mother this child, then she would just have to go to the local thrift store and buy herself one of those secondhand dolls that had been so popular with kids a few years ago. Even if she knew in her heart that no doll would begin to fill the emptiness inside of her—not like having Allison back would.

In that moment Whitney knew for certain she should just get in her car and race away from the man and the child. But instead, she found herself rooted to the spot, her eyes straying once again to where her neighbor still stood. She watched as he opened the rear door to his Jeep and began loading his purchases into the back of the vehicle. Suddenly the bottom of a plastic bag he'd lifted from the cart ruptured, spilling on the parking lot canned goods that rolled in every possible direction. Thinking she heard him give a low curse, Whitney found herself grinning as she lifted her eyebrows a fraction higher than normal.

She continued to observe the somewhat comical scene for several more seconds before finally deciding to give the guy a hand. After all, what could it hurt? He was her neighbor, for heaven's sake. They lived less than two hundred feet apart. They'd have to meet sooner or later.

"Hi," Whitney called out in a peppy tone of voice as she moved closer, a smile inching its way up her face. "Looks like you could use some help."

Scowling, her new neighbor jerked piercing green eyes in her direction, and for a moment Whitney felt the ground beneath her waver. His thick eyebrows burrowed into a deeper frown. "No, that's okay. I can handle it," he practically barked out. Then, turning back to his task, he added in a less curt tone of voice, "But thanks, just the same."

He squatted down and began recovering the canned goods that had rolled under his Jeep and placing them inside another bag. Whitney looked down and saw a couple of cans near her feet. Shrugging off his thanks-but-no-thanks, she picked up one in each hand. When he stood and turned toward his cart, she offered them to him. He peered at her for a long moment through narrowed, compelling eyes. Finally he took them with a grudgingly given "Thanks."

"Don't mention it."

He pivoted and walked to the front of his Jeep, where another can had rolled near the front left tire, all the while keeping an eye on the little girl, who was still seated in the grocery cart. Whitney watched him scoop up the can of chicken noodle soup before her gaze switched to the child. Dear God, but she couldn't have stopped herself from looking in that direction, not even if she'd been paid to. Allison's sudden disappearance from her life had left a huge void inside her that so desperately needed to be filled, and it didn't matter how hard and how often she told herself otherwise.

Smiling, she leaned forward and said, "Hi there, sweetie. What's your name?"

Her neighbor walked right up behind her. "I'm teaching her not to speak to strangers," he said.

"That's a good idea," Whitney said, agreeing with him wholeheartedly. But inwardly she couldn't help wondering how such a sweet-looking child could have such a grumpy grizzly-bear-of-a-father.

On the heels of that thought she suddenly became aware of the warmth of the male body so close to her own, and smelled the clean, spicy scent of his aftershave. She knew if she turned around to face him that her nose would probably graze his blue cotton shirt. Why, he was practically on top of her—well, not exactly on top....

And not that she cared about—or wanted—such a thing!

Still, much to her distress, she found he remained much too close. She couldn't think clearly and had to frantically search her brain for her next coherent words.

"But I'm not *really* a stranger," she finally managed. Taking a step to the side, she drew in a deep breath before spinning around to offer him her outstretched hand. "I'm Whitney Sue Arceneaux. I live across the street from you."

His eyes widened a degree, and Whitney felt certain that her unexpected introduction had startled him. She smiled to herself. Now that he knew who she was, he would undoubtedly stumble over an apology for not recognizing her sooner. His tone of voice would become friendlier. His full, sexy mouth would lift in a wondrous smile. The golden flecks in his angry gaze would disappear, and his eyes would become as green as the rice fields of Acadia Parish. He would tell her his name in that deep, sexy voice— Oh, for heaven's sake, why was her heart pounding so madly? No need of a respirator for this fool, she told herself as she suddenly realized that some wayward—*wanton*—part of her could hardly wait to hear the husky, sexy sound of his voice again.

"Oh, yeah," he replied, gazing directly into her eyes without any evidence of the smile she'd imagined spreading across his handsome face. Had she ever looked into eyes so compelling, so volatile?

He planted his feet apart and placed his wide hands on his hips, hands that were connected to bronzed, corded forearms. "*Now* I remember you," he said, nodding slowly. "You're the one from across the street. You're often standing in your yard when I return from work in the afternoons. Sometimes I see you in the mornings, too. You must not have much to do."

"I like being outdoors," Whitney replied in self-defense, caught off guard. She turned beet red as a swift embarrassment flooded her face. Good grief, the man was intimidating.

Without meeting his eyes she said, "And actually, I—I'm a very busy person."

Nervously licking her lips and wishing she'd never come over to help him in the first place, she turned her attention back to the little girl and smiled. "She's precious. Is she your daughter?"

"Look, Ms. . . ."

"Arceneaux," she said, supplying her last name for him. She glanced at him momentarily, then turned back to the child. She certainly didn't want him thinking that she was interested in him. That was the last thing she wanted. Because she wasn't. Not in *that* way. Not in any way.

"Look, Ms. Arceneaux, I don't mean to be rude, but I'm sort of in a hurry to get home. I'm expecting an important phone call and I've already been delayed much too long. So if you don't mind, I'd like to be on my way." Having said that, he excused himself, unfastened the safety strap holding his child in place and lifted the little girl from the grocery cart. He settled her in the baby's special car seat.

According to her book of etiquette, Whitney felt she'd been rudely dismissed. Without uttering another word, she turned to go.

What a jerk, she told herself minutes later as she drove home. At a red light she glanced at herself in the rearview mirror and saw she was still flushed from the encounter. Her new neighbor was a total jerk. Why, the man didn't even possess the common courtesy necessary to introduce himself.

This time, when she retrieved her groceries from her car, she didn't so much as glance across the street. Hah! She'd show him. She had a lot more important things to do with her time than worry about him and his child. And whatever motherly instinct she'd felt for his child could be smothered easily with just one snap of her fingers.

And no doubt the quicker she snapped them, the better off she'd be in the long run.

But Garrett Scott, alias Garrett Wilson, had seen when his neighbor returned from the supermarket and marched into her house like a drill sergeant. Damn it! The last thing he'd wanted to do was to get her upset.

Aw, the heck with her, he thought, though the tightening in his gut told him he really felt otherwise. An angry, nosy neighbor was the last thing he and Elsbeth needed right now. Nosy neighbors would eventually ask nosy questions. And nosy questions would lead to answers he couldn't give. Not to her. Not to anyone. All he wanted was for him and Elsbeth to be able to blend quietly into mainstream society without an ounce of gossip aimed at them. He'd hoped to accomplish that by keeping to himself. Which was why he wished the cute little redhead from across the street would mind her own business and leave him alone.

Maybe he was simply overreacting.

Lord knows, it wasn't his first time, and from the way his life was going these days, it probably wasn't going to be his last. He'd been looking over his shoulder ever since he and Elsbeth had left San Francisco four months ago. Overreacting was just part of the anxiety that gnawed at his gut.

"Da-da," Elsbeth said as he carried her into the house. "Cookie."

It hadn't taken his daughter long to learn that she would get a treat each time they returned home. She was a bright little kid for a sixteen-month-old and as sweet as the honey graham cracker he handed her. She was his life.

As if she'd read his thoughts, she took a small bite and gave him an easy grin, showing off the few baby teeth that had grown in.

"That's Daddy's good little girl. One bite at a time," Garrett said.

Walking into her bedroom, he dropped her diaper bag on the side of the small bed she slept in and then placed her and a small stuffed panda bear inside its railings. After winding up a couple of her mechanical toys to entertain her, he went into his bedroom to change from the pair of blue jeans he wore to an old pair of cutoffs and an even older T-shirt that had had the sleeves ripped out. He watched Elsbeth through the open doorway.

As he quickly undressed, he noticed in the mirror that his back and chest were tanned, his muscles leaner and firmer than they'd been in a long time. He was an architect by profession and usually he sat behind a desk or drawing table for hours at a time. During the past ten years, exercising was something he'd done at a health club after five o'clock and on weekends. But for the past four months he had been doing the same kind of construction work that he'd done during his college days. He'd taken odd jobs wherever he could find them on the escape route that he'd taken from California, and the hard labor had strengthened his body in a way that no amount of sit-ups or bench presses had been able to accomplish. He liked the change.

But mostly he liked the fact that the employers in construction didn't ask very many questions. As long as a person did what he was told, he was left alone. And that's what Garrett wanted more than any other benefit they could offer him. Later on, if he decided it was safe to settle down in any one spot for very long, he would make up a résumé and look for something more permanent. Actually he'd hoped that this small neighborhood on the outskirts of Baton Rouge would turn out to be a good place for him and Elsbeth to stay for a while. But now with the nosy neighbor breathing down his neck, he wasn't so sure if it was such a good idea to remain in this one place much longer.

Damn. Now why in the hell didn't she find herself another pastime besides his business?

After the episode in the parking lot, Whitney huffed and puffed around her house for an hour or so, her thoughts mostly on the infuriating man across the street. He had intentionally intimidated her. But why?

And why should she care if he wanted to go around acting like a jerk? Telling herself she didn't, she dressed in a pair of old white shorts and a yellow T-shirt, which she twisted into a knot under her breasts. She went outside to work in her garden. It wouldn't be long now before her flower beds would be blooming with caladiums, periwinkles, lantana and roses.

Whitney's street was part of an older subdivision on the outskirts of Baton Rouge. The houses were made of wood, with enclosed garages, front porches and latticework. The late-twenty, early-thirty-something generation was buying the houses and modernizing them to accommodate their young, growing families. A few residents, like Whitney, were single, but married or not, they had all become close friends and joined together to make their block a fun place to live.

The weather was great today, and everyone was outdoors. Gazing up, Whitney saw that several huge, lazy white puff clouds dotted the endless blue sky. Temperatures would probably rise to eighty-five degrees by midafternoon. She recalled the publicized warnings about using a sunscreen and went back inside to apply a rich coconut-scented lotion to her skin.

When she emerged once again, she was still barefoot. And while she'd placed a white sweatband around her head, after only five minutes of pulling weeds from her flower beds, perspiration began to trickle down the sides of her face.

About thirty minutes later she was engrossed in getting her yard cleaned up when she heard the sound of the mailman's truck approaching. Standing and stretching out the muscles in her back, she pulled off her work gloves and watched the small vehicle roll down the street. Slowly she began walking toward the road, knowing her mailman would be at her stop soon. She noticed that he quickly scooted past her new neighbor's mailbox without stopping, before going on to each subsequent box on his route. Having reached the end of the street, he made a U-turn and started up her side. He stopped at the Erwin house first, then he eased up to hers.

"G'morning, Whitney," he said, handing her the mail he had for her.

"Good morning, Charlie," she replied with a smile. "Nice day, for a change."

"Sure is."

Charlie moved on, and Whitney walked back toward her house to deposit her mail inside.

She loved the small framed house she'd purchased a few years ago. She'd bought it from an elderly couple who wanted to retire to the country to be near their son. The exterior had been freshly painted as part of the sale agreement, so Whitney's remodeling had basically consisted of a fresh paint job in each of the seven rooms, which included a kitchen, a small dining room, a parlor, two bedrooms, one bath and a utility room. Her careful use of the latest in color trends had done wonders for the forty-year-old interior. After moving in, she found she needed more overhead lighting in the kitchen and had a new light fixture installed. She had other ideas for modernizing the little house, but for now she was content with it.

She walked into the dining room and laid her mail on the table, scattering it so she could get a better look at it. That was when she noticed that all the sales brochures and flyers that Charlie had handed her were duplicated. She separated them and was about to drop the extra set in the trash can in the kitchen when she noticed that the address read Current Resident, 104 Shady Place.

Her address was 105 Shady Place.

Charlie had given her the sales brochures that should have been delivered to the address of her new neighbor across the street.

"Oh, well," she said aloud. "Nobody actually sits down and reads these things, anyway. I'm sure he won't miss them."

Dropping them into the trash, she headed back outside. She was on the last step down when she began to wonder whether she should have thrown his mail away like that. With a shake of her head, she decided she'd done the right thing and went back to weeding her flower beds.

But fifteen minutes later she found herself retrieving the sales information from her trash can. Then, marching herself into the bathroom, she began to clean up. After all, she couldn't very well bring her new grizzly-bear-of-a-neighbor his mail when she looked like she'd been bathing the family pet in an outdoor washtub.

And surely it was her duty to bring the man his mail. It might have taken her a while to realize that, but now that she had, she was going to walk right across the street and hand over those brochures to him. After all, she was an honest, law-abiding citizen, and everyone knew that tampering with the U.S. mail was a federal offense. Besides, it was only right that her new neighbor get his mail.

After brushing her hair and pinning her long bangs to the back of her head with a gold-tone barrette, she patted her cheeks, which for some reason were already flushed—probably the leftovers from their earlier encounter that morning. Pressing her lips together to smear the cherry-flavored lip gloss she put on, Whitney slipped her feet into a pair of white leather sandals. Why she was going to so much trouble was beyond her comprehension. Wild and angry predators such as grizzly bears didn't usually take the time to distinguish friend from foe—they attacked first. And besides, she'd probably be downwind from him and he wouldn't catch her scent, good or bad, just as he never seemed to see her, even when he looked in her direction.

That thought had her marching to where she had left *his* mail on one corner of the kitchen cabinet, not giving herself another single second to reconsider what she was doing. She figured her nerve was going to last her only so long. Therefore, each moment was of critical importance here; after all, if she ran out of guts when she rang his doorbell, what in the world would she do if he answered it?

That embarrassing thought almost made her turn around.

Almost.

Jim, her next-door neighbor, was mowing his front lawn when Whitney stepped from her front porch and strutted across the street. She felt his eyes focused on her the whole time and figured before this episode in her life was over, he and his wife, Samantha—who also just happened to be her best friend—would know all about it. At that particular moment, Whitney wished she lived on a deserted street that had only two houses, hers and the one she steadily approached. She climbed the steps, rang the doorbell and then cleared her throat, hoping that her voice would sound normal when she spoke. That was, if she had the chance to speak. Several moments had already ticked by and, as of yet, *he* hadn't answered the door.

After a minute or so the color of jaundice began creeping over her, and she thought she might just hurry back over to her place before she started to look like a summer squash. That was when she heard the door creak open—but only a few inches.

"Can I help you?" came the familiar masculine voice that could only belong to her bear-of-a-neighbor. It was still as deep and rich and gruff as it had been when she'd spoken to him in the parking lot.

Fe-fi-fo-fum! I smell the blood of an Englishman. Grrr.

Don't lose your nerve, she told herself.

"Uh...y-yes...remember me, from this morning?" she inquired hesitantly. "I...uh...well, actually...

the mailman accidently placed some of your mail in my box.''

''I don't get any mail.''

''Not at all?'' Whitney blurted out, more from surprise than curiosity. What kind of a man didn't get *any* mail?

A mysterious man.

She licked her dry lips. He still hadn't opened the door any more than a few inches, maybe five at the most.

''I mean, I don't get any mail at this address. But to be perfectly honest, I don't think that's any of your business. Now, if you'll excuse me . . .''

That *excuse me* was almost the same kind of line that he had used to dismiss her in the parking lot. Why was it that most men—like her manipulative brother-in-law—could so easily dismiss her?

Whitney was determined that this time would be different. After all, she had a legitimate, law-abiding reason for having come over, didn't she? Still, she felt her nerve slipping a notch or two. ''Well, this stuff is addressed to 104 Shady Place. I happen to know that's your house number, but I'm sorry to have bothered you.'' She turned to leave, but halted when she heard the door squeak open.

''Ms. Arceneaux?''

She whirled around and blinked twice in disbelief. He had actually stepped through the doorway and onto the porch! She was immediately mesmerized by the intensity of his green gaze. ''Yes?'' she finally managed, though her throat felt tight, as though it were freezing up on her.

''I'll take what you have that's mine.''

Suddenly she felt she couldn't breathe—or walk—or talk. The truth was she felt as though she were being swept away.

But not this time, she told herself. Oh *no*. This time she was a whole lot smarter about life and wasn't about to fall victim to another heartache. The pain of losing her sister and Allison was still too raw. It would always be too raw. Once upon a time she might have been silly enough to dream of finding her very own Prince Charming, just as all little girls do. But that had been a long time ago. Long before Lisa's death. Long before she'd realized that her father would never quite love her as much as he had loved Lisa. And long before her brother-in-law had taken unfair advantage of her kindness.

But no more. She told herself firmly that she couldn't have cared less if this guy continued to look at her as though it pained him to even speak in her direction; as though, if her foot had indeed fit the glass slipper from one of her favorite childhood fairy tales, he would have smashed it to smithereens before allowing *her* to try it on.

She thrust the mail into his outstretched hand and spun around again to leave, praying her knees wouldn't buckle beneath her. When she reached her front porch she turned almost against her will and saw that he was still standing in his doorway, watching her.

Damn you, Mister Whoever-You-Are. *You're* no Prince Charming, that's for sure. She walked inside and slammed shut her front door.

And for crying out loud, what modern-day woman would want such a ridiculous-looking, fairy-tale character in her life, anyway?

She sure didn't.

Chapter Two

Garrett had watched his nosy neighbor sashay herself back across the street to her house, and they had stared each other down from their respective front porches. She had looked as though she were ready to spit nails at him. Well, it wasn't his fault she was sticking her pretty little upturned nose where she had no business!

Actually, after the way he'd acted toward her in the parking lot this morning, she really had some nerve to come over and ring his doorbell as though she was unaware of his wish to be left alone. Was she blind?

Aw, the hell with it, he said to himself. Just why did she have to come along with her wide, innocent smile and add to his overload of problems? A second later he slammed his own front door, and Elsbeth looked up from where she sat in her high chair with round, startled eyes. He walked over and poured milk into her drinking cup, then snapped on the lid.

One thing was for certain about that woman. She could end up being big trouble for him if he didn't keep her at bay. Never mind that at times he found himself standing near the front window, looking out as she steadily did the gardening in her front yard, unaware she was being watched. Never mind that when he did, he often experienced a deep yearning for something he knew he'd lost somewhere along the way.

"I even dreamed about her the other night," he mumbled out loud, as though that would ease the guilt he felt for having been so rude to her at the door. "Can you imagine that, Elsbeth? I actually dreamed about the woman. She was selling smiles at the state fair. Three for a dollar." He shook his dark head as though he couldn't believe the absurdity of his own dream. "And I bought twenty dollars' worth."

Elsbeth grinned and then picked up her clear plastic drinking cup and sucked on the spout. Milk ran down the corners of her mouth and was soaked up by the blue terry-cloth bib tied around her neck.

"That a girl, Lissy," Garrett said, coaxing her to eat the lunch he'd prepared for her. Delighting in his praise, she took another swallow.

Watching the contented expression on her small, round face formed a lump in Garrett's throat the size of a golf ball. His life might have been in shambles, but at least his daughter was safe, and for him that was the most important thing. Someday this nightmare would end. God, he just hoped it was soon.

Unfortunately, for now it was a useless wish, and no one knew that better than he did. His ex-in-laws weren't the kind of people who backed down when they wanted something as much as they claimed to want his daughter. But they couldn't have her, damn it. Not if he could help it.

For him, life on the run was pure hell. Besides the constant fear of being discovered, there was the loneliness, the sense of isolation that surrounded him at all times. He watched as everyone around him went about their daily lives. They never seemed to stop to consider what might happen if their worlds were suddenly turned upside down as his had been.

And fortunately for most, they would never have to think about it because their lives would remain the same, day after day, year after year. Stability, his parents had called it, and that was the environment in which they had raised their two sons. Until now Garrett had never realized just how much that way of life had become a necessary part of him.

Elsbeth banged her spoon on the hard white plastic tray that held her secure in her high chair. Garrett looked over at her and with a slow shake of his head resigned himself to the fact that he was going to have to do something about her hair. While most kids her age were still slightly bald, Elsbeth's thick mop of brown hair was hanging in her eyes. Its color and silky texture reminded him a lot of his mother's hair before it had turned gray with age.

Then he remembered the pack of different-colored barrettes he'd purchased at the grocery that morning, and picked up the cardboard holder from where he'd placed it on the counter, removing a red plastic heart-shaped one. Using his fingers, he combed back his daughter's long bangs and gathered them so he could slip the bottom part of the barrette beneath them. His big fingers felt clumsy and got in his way when he tried to snap the clip shut. By the time his task was completed, there were very few strands of Elsbeth's brown hair being held in the barrette's grasp.

Garrett, however, felt pleased with himself and stepped back to admire his accomplishment as Elsbeth began to shake her head from side to side.

"No, no, no," she chanted happily, banging the metal spoon against the food tray, a sound that Garrett had grown almost accustomed to hearing at mealtimes. But his moment of pleasure was short-lived; he watched in wide-eyed disbelief as the red barrette slipped from her hair and fell to the floor.

Frustrated, he picked it up and tried again. Only this time Elsbeth ignored his quiet command to hold still. So, after several more failed attempts to arrange her hair with the contraption, he gave up and pitched it into a basket of miscellaneous junk on the table. Maybe he'd have to think of something else to do with her hair. Maybe he'd have to think about giving her bangs a trim.

He ate the ham-and-cheese sandwich he'd prepared before his nosy neighbor had shown up, then he went out back and set up Elsbeth's playpen on the patio. After placing her inside, he began to clear out the weeds from the small garden that had been left by the previous residents. The tall redwood fence that surrounded the backyard gave him the privacy he desired.

On a whim he'd bought a couple of tomato plants from the nursery down the road and he intended to plant them in the garden. He knew there was a good chance that he wouldn't be here to see them bear fruit, but just the thought of watching them grow was enough for now. Somehow it made him feel a bit more human, a bit more like the small-town boy he'd once been. Someday he was going to have a vegetable garden the size of this whole

damned backyard, he vowed inwardly. Someday his life
was going to be normal again. He had to believe that.

The following days were busy ones for Whitney,
though not quite busy enough to keep her thoughts from
straying, every now and then, to the man and child living across the street from her. At times she found herself gazing out the window, wondering about them.

She'd placed a classified in Sunday's newspaper, ad-
vertising her in-home accounting services, and she was
swamped with calls on Monday. She had room for only
two new clients and found them both by Tuesday morning.

On Wednesday she happened to glance up while eat-
ing breakfast, and saw her reclusive neighbor and his
child driving away. Her silly heart—like the fool it had
proven to be—took off like a quarter horse after them,
but fortunately for her own sense of pride, its speed was
no match for the Jeep Cherokee.

By Saturday morning Whitney was ready to go outdoors and spend most of the day in the sun. She mowed
her lawn and then used her Weed Eater lawn trimmer to
trim the tall grass in the odd places she couldn't reach
with her mower. The only time she stopped and went
inside was to boil potatoes and eggs for the salad she was
preparing for the neighborhood get-together that was
being held later at the Erwins' house. It would be a fun
party; she was sure of it. Everyone on the block, young
and old, recent or old-timers to the neighborhood, was
invited. Even the grizzly bear had gotten an invitation.

Would he come?

Probably not, she answered herself. And when Samantha Erwin came over around three o'clock to bor-
row all the ice Whitney could spare from her freezer, she

confirmed Whitney's suspicions. He had already declined by telephone earlier in the week. Samantha said she thought it was because he was shy and didn't want to come alone. She wanted Whitney to go over later that afternoon and offer to bring him along with her as a guest. Whitney had told her best friend that she was crazy if she thought their new neighbor was shy. In the end Samantha had told her to think about her request, and Whitney had said, "No way."

But now it was all she seemed to be able to think about.

Yet, in all seriousness, wasn't it for the best if he didn't go? she kept asking herself. Who wanted to have to deal with an angry bear all night long? Never mind that Samantha *might* have been right about the guy. Never mind that he probably didn't have many friends, just as Samantha had surmised. He was a grown man, for heaven's sake. His personality quirks weren't her problem. Besides, was there such a thing as a shy grizzly?

Nope, she didn't think so. Samantha had him pegged all wrong.

At four-thirty Whitney watered the small crop of parsley growing in the large clay flowerpot near her back steps, then called it quits for the day and went inside to clean up. After showering, she examined the white cotton skirt and green-striped blouse she was going to wear to the barbecue and decided both needed pressing.

For the most part, clothes weren't a big deal to her. She had enough problems just trying to decide what to do with her stubborn hair. It was baby fine, but thick, and never cooperated with the way she wanted to style it. Today was certainly no different for the rich, arrogant strands that she'd inherited from her Scots-Irish grandmother. After attempting to arrange it in several different ways that only ended in total frustration for her, she finally gave up and just allowed it to do whatever—heaven help her—it wanted.

She finished dressing and went into the kitchen to ice down a couple of bottles of light beer that she wanted to bring with her to the party. Then, balancing the bowl of potato salad in one hand, she tucked the small blue-and-white ice chest containing her two beers under her arm and pulled open the back door with her free hand.

She immediately heard the sounds of laughter and music coming from next door. She noticed the gray smoke from the barbecue pit that floated over the twenty-year-old red-tipped hedges separating her property from the Erwins'. The scrumptious smell of seasoned, roasting chicken made her stomach growl with hunger. In the next moment she heard Samantha's voice urging the newlyweds from down the street to come on in and make themselves at home.

Smiling, she headed around the corner of her house with the intention of hurrying over to join them. But instead, she found herself pausing on her front lawn, her gaze shifting to the white-painted house across the street.

It had been a week since her encounter with her new neighbor, and she still felt flushed when she thought of him—which was more often than she cared to admit. The image of his face, it seemed, was constantly lurking in the outer reaches of her mind. Would she ever be able to forget the intensity of those green eyes?

She feared not.

Was she really going to allow his poor attitude to stop her from being the friendly person she should be? What if he really *was* shy? Maybe his grizzly personality was nothing more than a self-defense mechanism.

Yeah, sure. And the sun sets in the east, too.

But what if he and his daughter really did need a friend? Could she really turn her back on them?

Did she dare do otherwise? After all, wasn't she just beginning to get her life back together since Allison had been taken from her?

She turned toward the Erwins' backyard. A burst of laughter rang out. The party was already in full swing. She glanced over her shoulder. And the grizzly bear from across the street and his child would miss all the fun.

Darn it. No one should expect this of her. Not Samantha. Not even herself.

And no one did.

So go on to the party, a small voice inside her said. *And have a good time.*

She would, she told herself. Only she wasn't quite able to convince herself to move in that direction.

Finally, sighing in resignation, she swung the personal-size cooler down to her side and tightened her other arm around the large bowl of potato salad. Then she started across the street.

You'll be sorry, her inner voice said. *He'll probably growl at you.* She ignored the warning and rang his doorbell, anyway. No one could call her a coward, by golly.

But after several long moments that gave him ample time to come to the door, she began to have second thoughts about what she was doing. However, it was too late to reconsider. The front door was finally opening.

"What is it this time, Ms. Arceneaux?" her neighbor said, sounding as though he were already irritated with her. But good grief, what had *she* done to him?

The arrogant so-and-so! Didn't he have the good sense to know she was doing this for his own good—and for his child's, as well? Whitney found herself trying to peek around him in the hopes of getting a glimpse of the little girl, but she didn't see anyone.

So, with a look of sheer willfulness, she glanced up and met his green eyes head-on. They were as stormy as a hurricane.

Then her gaze slowly slipped down the length of him, and she suddenly found herself gaping. Sweet heaven, did he ever look magnificent in a pair of worn cutoff jean shorts that hung down an inch below his navel! The white cutoff T-shirt he wore didn't do much to cover his very masculine chest, either. In fact, the lack of white fabric did nothing more than flaunt the tornado of dark curly hair that tunneled toward the waistband of his cutoffs. My goodness . . . he was *half-naked*. At least about as naked as she cared to see him—which, of course, was something of a lie and she knew it—because in the next moment she found herself wishing she could come up with a good reason to have him lift his arms above his head. That way she could see even more of his lean-muscled body. But unless he suddenly decided to make a quick swipe for the mosquito buzzing over their heads, that was unlikely.

Too bad. Her face flushed even hotter at the realization that she wanted to see it all, every single inch of him. He'd rolled up the sleeves of the T-shirt, and they emphasized the strong, corded muscles in his arms. As she continued to stare, her gaze lingering longer than necessary on certain strategic areas of his body—like the indentation of his navel—a slow but noisy growl spiraled through her stomach. Yeah, she was starving, all right, but not for anything that would require the help of amino acids to be digested.

Well, she told herself with a start back to reality, at least she had something to celebrate. He had actually remembered her last name. Hip-hip-hooray! Where was the drum roll? she thought sarcastically.

Feeling a sudden surge of self-confidence, she swallowed hard and tried hanging on to every ounce of it. "And a good day to you, too, neighbor," she replied with a cheerfulness she didn't really feel. She only felt hot, but she wasn't going to let *him* know that. And just for her own benefit, Whitney reminded herself that this was the *very* last time she was going to try to be friendly, child or no child. Samantha or no Samantha.

"Look, I'm busy. Have you come over here again to give me more mail?"

"N-no—not this time," she stammered, inwardly chastising herself for doing so.

There she was, intimidated by him—again. Some self-confidence she had.

"Uh...actually...well...look, I just thought maybe you'd like to attend tonight's neighborhood barbecue." She turned and pointed toward Samantha and Jim's house, which by now was all lit up. "I happen to know you refused the invitation earlier in the week, but Samantha—the hostess—well, she thinks it's because you're new in the neighborhood and might be a bit shy. Of course, I told her I didn't think so."

Now why had she said that, for land's sake?

Garrett almost smiled. Almost. Then his face went carefully blank. "Well, you're right. My being shy has nothing to do with it. I'm just not the sociable type, that's all."

"Oh, I can tell that," Whitney agreed emphatically before stopping to consider how she must sound to him. Her handsome new neighbor stared at her for just a second, and then suddenly something miraculous happened. He smiled. It started at the corners of his full

mouth and didn't end until he was showing off a set of
beautiful white teeth that were in striking contrast to his
deep tan. And just as it had at the parking lot when his
eyes had met hers for the first time, the earth beneath
Whitney's feet wavered.

"See. The big bad wolf does smile after all," he said,
still grinning at her.

"Grizzly," Whitney corrected.

"What?"

"I called you a grizzly," she said, biting back her own
silly grin. Gracious, this change in his attitude was too
much, too soon. She knew that leopards didn't change
their spots, and grizzlies didn't dull their claws, so what
would his next move be?

"A grizzly, am I?"

"Well..."

"Actually I think I'm more the teddy bear type."

If Whitney had been wearing a pair of false teeth, she
would have swallowed them. Talk about true colors! The
man's image of himself was so distorted he didn't even
know the truth when it was spelled out to him. Teddy
bear, indeed.

She looked up and saw the amused glint in his green
eyes as he studied her. Yup. A true predator if ever she
saw one. Just like an old grizzly.

He cleared his throat. "Look, I guess I've gotten us
off to a bad start. Could we try again?"

Amazingly, Garrett found himself standing perfectly
still, holding his breath while waiting for her answer. He
frowned when he saw her brows draw together.

Now why did she always have to look so disappointed
in him? And why had she been appointed the neighborhood's guardian angel?

Probably, he thought, because she *did* resemble an angel, at least sort of. That was providing angels had thick, silky red hair that looked as though it had been styled by a Kansas tornado.

Cute. She was definitely cute. There was something earthy about her—long legs, nice breasts. Her full, sensual mouth almost dominated her other facial features. No doubt she was the type who would have an herb garden growing in her backyard. She would like babies and hamsters and homemade apple pie.

With a mental jerk Garrett put a stop to his wayward thoughts. If there was one thing he knew about himself, it was that he couldn't have his pie and eat it, too. Just get rid of her, his inner voice said. And make it quick. She's getting to you, and if that isn't bad enough, you're beginning to like it.

Ridiculous, he argued back. It was just that he'd been alone for the past four months and a little bit of female attention made him feel as if his life was…well…normal again.

"I don't think there are any rules against neighbors starting over," Whitney finally said, breaking into another smile.

"Well…" Garrett said, hesitating just a moment. "I guess you're right. My name's Garrett Scott—uh… Wilson." For the first time since he'd been on the move, Garrett hated having to use the alias he had tagged on to his name. Suddenly he felt as though he was betraying his heritage, not to mention the woman standing there before him with a nice, friendly smile on her face.

"Well, I guess there's no need to introduce myself again. Undoubtedly you know who I am by now," Whitney replied.

He stuck out a callused hand. "Whitney Arceneaux, right?" She nodded. "Pleased to meet you."

Whitney slipped her hand into his. "Same here," she replied, feeling a quickening of her heartbeat. Her name from his lips had sounded so... so... sexy. Her smaller hand now cocooned in his larger one felt so... so... consumed.

The grizzly was most definitely capable of carrying a dainty glass slipper in his paw, if need be.

Whitney felt breathless and yet so completely alive it was as though a rocket had gone off inside her, sending small flickers of life throughout her body. "Do come to the party. I know you'll have a great time. Besides, Samantha will never forgive me if I fail to get you there."

"This Samantha sounds like a real character."

"She's a gem. Oh, sometimes she can be overbearing, but her husband, Jim, is about as down-to-earth as anyone can get. He keeps her on an even keel. They make a terrific pair." She smiled at the thought of her friends. She was lucky to have them.

Garrett found himself smiling back as he ran a quick hand through his hair. Sighing, he suddenly decided to totally ignore his common sense. After all, maybe his method of trying to "disappear" was all wrong. Instead of keeping himself and Elsbeth apart from everyday life, maybe he needed to become a joiner, to blend in with humanity. "It'll take me a few minutes to get my daughter and myself ready. Do you mind waiting?"

"Me? No, of course not. I'm in no hurry," Whitney said with a casual wave of her hand. But the sudden rosy blush to her cheeks gave away her true reaction to this new, sudden change in him. Still, she couldn't help but be somewhat pleased with herself. After all, she *had* convinced him to go to the party. Maybe, just maybe she was a bit more charming than she gave herself credit for. But whatever the reason for his change of mind, she was more than willing to sacrifice the necessary time it would take for him and his child to get ready for the party. Besides, now that she'd come this far, she certainly wasn't going to leave him on his own. Why, he could very well change his mind again once she was on her way and never walk over to join her and the others! No siree. She wasn't leaving without him.

"Can I help you with something?" she asked, her thoughts adding impetus to the offer. "What I mean is, I could help with your daughter, if you like."

"Her name's Elsbeth," he said.

"That's pretty," Whitney replied.

"It was my grandmother's name."

"She's really a darling little girl."

One side of Garrett's mouth lifted slightly. "She looks a lot like my mother."

"Oh?" Whitney said, unaware she'd lifted her eyebrows. "And what about her mother? Does Elsbeth look anything like her?"

"A little around the mouth, I think."

"Oh, I see," Whitney replied, suddenly wishing he'd given her a bit more information about the woman. For instance, her whereabouts, not to mention her current role in his life.

He must have read her mind. Clearing his throat, he said, "But we're divorced now, and I have custody of Elsbeth."

"Oh, I see," Whitney replied, hating the fact that her brain couldn't seem to put together anything larger than a three-word sentence.

And why should she care if he was divorced, married or single? It wasn't as if it was going to make a big difference to her. They were neighbors, that was all.

"Well, we're into the nineties and all, but a man having sole custody of his small child is still a bit of an oddity in these parts. It kind of makes you stand out in a crowd, if you know what I mean."

Garrett's gut tightened. God only knew, that was the last thing he wanted. He narrowed his eyes and for a moment looked more like a grizzly than even he intended. "Are you saying that Elsbeth and I stand out in a crowd?"

"Uh . . . yeah," Whitney replied, mesmerized by the intensity of his hypnotic gaze. "You could say that. I mean . . . well . . ." Oh, God, she thought, blinking twice to break the momentary spell. She desperately wanted to back away from this conversation; the man looked ready to pounce and devour anyone who disagreed with him. So why wasn't Samantha the one standing here, taking the emotional roller-coaster ride that Whitney felt she was on? Wasn't this bubble-brained idea all hers in the first place? "Look, it's just that your behavior . . . well . . . it hasn't exactly been friendly, if you know what I mean. That makes you somewhat of an oddity in this neighborhood and only fuels everyone's curiosity even more."

"Are you saying that if I become my most charming self tonight at the party that the neighbors will be less concerned with me?"

"Probably," Whitney said with an assured nod.

Apparently satisfied with her answer, he switched topics. "Tell me, Whitney, have you lived in this subdivision very long?"

"A couple of years. I bought my house from a retired couple."

"You're not married?" he asked in a way that implied he already knew the answer.

"No, I'm not." Darn it. She was still using those three-word sentences. "I've never been married," she elaborated quickly.

Which was, of course, the truth. Yet in all honesty, during the three years that she'd cared for her brother-in-law and her niece, she *had* felt like a wife and mother. Not in the intimate sense, of course, but emotionally she had been as good as married. And along with all the other feelings of hurt, she'd felt betrayed when her brother-in-law had suddenly taken off.

"Well," Garrett said, clearing his throat, "I guess I'd better get ready if we're going to make it to the party. And thanks for offering to help, but I can manage to dress Elsbeth by myself. Just have a seat," he said, waving her in and closing the door behind her. "I won't be long."

"Sure," Whitney replied. "I'll just wait right here in the kitchen."

He nodded, then turned and began gathering some papers that he'd spread out on the kitchen counter. He scanned them closely, as though making sure that nothing was out of the ordinary. Then apparently satisfied, he left the room.

Whitney placed the ice chest she'd been carrying on the floor and the bowl of potato salad on the table. In Garrett's wake she surveyed the room with a quick glance. Finding nothing unusual or out of place, she shrugged and sat down in an oak straight-back chair at the dinette table.

It was several long minutes before she heard any sound coming from the part of the house where Garrett had disappeared. But when she finally did, she heard Garrett telling his daughter to sit still while he combed her hair. A second later she heard a childish squeal that ended with a fit of giggles.

Smiling at the innocent sound, a bittersweet pang of regret centered itself in Whitney's chest. Allison had been a happy child, too. Was she still?

Whitney took a deep breath and rose. Now wasn't the time to allow the past to creep in. If she did, her whole night would be ruined. She walked into the den and gazed out the patio doors for several long moments. When she turned back, Garrett was standing in the doorway, one of his sinewy arms cradled around his daughter, who seemed perfectly content in her perched position on his hip. In his other hand, he held a pink hairbrush. For some reason, every nerve in Whitney's body sprang to life.

"Look, do you know anything about barrettes?" he asked, his tone of voice sounding totally frustrated.

"Barrettes?" Whitney asked, walking toward him.

"Yeah, you know, barrettes," he said, repositioning something in his palm that was red and heart shaped and about two inches long. "Like this."

Whitney glanced down at what he held and smiled. "Is a Cajun French?"

"I beg your pardon?"

"Never mind," she said, waving aside her misunderstood joke. He didn't know it but she had just learned something more about him. He wasn't from around this area, or he would have caught on to what she'd meant.

By this time Garrett had walked farther into the kitchen and Whitney had taken several steps in his direction. When they both halted, they were only a few feet apart. She immediately noticed that he and his daughter both smelled like baby powder. To his credit, Whitney figured he had just sprinkled the little girl with a good dose of talc.

"Da-da," Elsbeth said, patting her father's face.

"Hi, there," Whitney said, reaching out to touch the child's finger. "Elsbeth, I think you and I are going to be good friends. Just you wait and see."

"Da-da," Elsbeth said, and then while closely observing Whitney, the child smacked her father on the cheek with a moist little kiss.

"Well, she certainly loves her daddy," Whitney said laughingly, yearning to take the child in her arms and squeeze her tight.

"Yeah," Garrett replied, gazing at his daughter. "We're a pair, all right."

His tone of voice sounded strange, as though the two of them were all alone in the world. Whitney felt her heart constrict. "What exactly do you want me to do with the barrette?"

"Clasp Elsbeth's bangs back from her face," Garrett replied, the hint of frustration returning to his voice. "They've grown so long that they hang down in her eyes. I don't know if they bother her any, but they're driving me plum crazy. Anyway, I can't seem to get this darn little thing to stay in her hair. Do you think you can?"

Whitney laughed softly. "I'd be willing to bet you just about anything that I can. Barrettes and bangs are my specialty. You probably didn't notice, but my hair has a mind of its own. I'm always trying to pin it up or down. Anything to make it behave."

They were standing close together now. Looking up, she saw he was grinning at her, showing a generous portion of even white teeth. The contrast was startling against his sun-kissed complexion. "And does it?" he asked, continuing to gaze down at her with those green eyes that seemed to glisten like bits of fire.

"Does it what?" she asked breathlessly, unable to look away from him. Why did she feel as though she was being seduced by a big, bad grizzly?

"Behave."

"My hair?"

"Uh-huh."

"Rarely."

"And how about you, Whitney? Do you always behave?"

Now she was sure of it. She couldn't breathe or think, but she could still feel because a rush of something warm and moist, something potent and out of control, was quickly spreading through her body.

The answer to his question didn't come to her in the form of words. It came to her slowly, starting not in her brain, but in the pit of her stomach. It slithered out in all directions, taunting her mercilessly until she knew the answer as well as she knew her own body.

She glanced up and found Garrett watching her through narrowed, probing eyes. Somehow she knew that every fiber in his body was aware of her every move, her every expression.

She knew something more. She was no match for the likes of this grizzly. Her best bet was to turn and run, but heaven help her, she couldn't even move. "I always behave," she finally managed to say.

A cocky grin crept up one side of his face as a sudden spark flared to life in his eyes. "Well, we just might have to do something to change that."

She went hot all over. Now, would Prince Charming have implied such a thing to Snow White?

Why, of course not.

But undoubtedly an old grizzly would have.

Chapter Three

As they stepped from Garrett's house, he placed his hand at the small of Whitney's back to usher her forward so he could close the door behind them. The simple contact caused her stomach to jackknife into her throat. For just a second she felt breathless again, but she chose to ignore it and started in the direction of the neighborhood barbecue, which already sounded as though it was in full swing.

Dressed in a lemon yellow polka-dot cotton playsuit, Elsbeth looked adorable in her father's arms. So that the barrette holding back the child's thick bangs would match her outfit, Whitney had exchanged the red heart-shaped barrette Garrett had handed to her for a yellow bow-shaped one that she'd found still attached to a cardboard holder. Then, right before leaving, Whitney had overcome the nagging fear that she was being presumptuous and had casually suggested that he remove the pink socks on Elsbeth's tiny feet and replace them with a pair of white ones.

"What's wrong with these?" he'd asked her. "They're brand-new."

"Take it from me, white socks would look much better," Whitney had replied.

"Really?"

"Really."

"Well...all right," Garrett had answered. Then, without further comment, he'd done as she bid.

And now they were walking side by side, heading across the street. "I'll carry the ice chest," he commanded, reaching down for the blue-and-white cooler. His big hand covered hers, causing an electrical jolt to zap through her body. He must have felt the power of it, too, because his gaze shot to her face.

Oh, for heaven's sake. He probably thought she was nuts.

And possibly he wasn't far from wrong.

"There's only a couple of beers in the cooler," Whitney exclaimed. "So it's not heavy." She tried to free the ice chest—and at the same time, her hand—from beneath his, but her efforts failed.

"Yeah, but I bet that bowl of potato salad you're carrying weighs plenty."

Again she attempted to free her trapped hand. "Not really," she replied quickly, feeling winded, as though she'd been out jogging for the past hour.

"I bet it does," he argued back. "And I just realized something else," he continued, as though he hadn't even noticed her slight struggle to get herself free of his grasp. "I should have brought my own refreshments, right?"

Whitney gave another tug, and this time she escaped, but found she had lost the battle to keep the ice chest in her possession. But, thank goodness, at least her hand was free. Why, another couple of seconds with his warm *paw* covering hers and she would have become totally senseless.

"No," she finally exclaimed, shaking her head. "There's always more than enough for everyone. Besides, this is your first time at one of our socials, so you're considered a guest." Then she suddenly thought of a way to get even with him for all the confusion he'd caused within her. She gazed up at him with a mischievous gleam in her eyes and said innocently, "I'll just tell everyone that you're insisting we have next month's party over at your house."

Garrett stopped in midstride and cut those gorgeous green eyes of his in her direction. "You're kidding, of course."

Whitney hadn't any doubts that she was staring into the most tantalizing gaze she had ever seen. Her heart began to bounce around in her chest. "Well, of course I'm kidding, Mr. Grizzly. Your constant growling would probably frighten everyone to death."

"Very funny," he said, now looking more relaxed and just a bit embarrassed by his quick response to something he'd just realized she'd meant as a joke. "I guess there's no point in my trying to convince you that my temperament is just the opposite of what you think it is?"

Whitney couldn't help herself as an easy grin lifted up both corners of her mouth. She was willing to bet that she knew *exactly* what his temperament was like. "Not on your life."

Reaching their destination, Whitney stopped at the wooden fence surrounding her neighbor's backyard. Because Garrett's hands were occupied, she opened the gate and waited while he stepped through, carrying Elsbeth and the ice chest.

For a moment no one seemed to notice their arrival. Then suddenly Samantha burst through the small group standing nearby and gave Whitney an exuberant hug. "I was beginning to worry that you weren't coming," she said loudly. Next to Whitney's ear, she whispered, "But now I see why you're late, you lucky dog."

Whitney felt certain that Garrett heard that comment and she made her immediate feelings toward her best friend quite clear by glowering at her. In turn, Samantha just raised her eyebrows at Whitney as if she didn't have the slightest idea what the problem could be.

Whitney held on to the bowl of potato salad with a death grip. The salad would have gone great with Sam's outfit. "Samantha Erwin, this is Garrett Wilson and his daughter, Elsbeth." Just at that moment Jim Erwin appeared, and Whitney immediately included him in the introduction. "Garrett, this is our host, Jim." The two men shook hands.

Samantha immediately turned toward the group and announced that Garrett and Elsbeth were the new neighbors who had moved in across the street from Whitney. Then she offered Garrett something to drink, and he graciously accepted a beer. Next she led him over to the table of appetizers. Whitney found her own way through the crowd.

Garrett thanked his hostess for her hospitality before offering a saltine cracker to his daughter. Then Samantha was called away from him to greet another couple. He continued to hold Elsbeth in place on his hip while telling himself to ignore the anxiety he felt growing within him. After all, this was his first real outing in months. Hell, probably the only one in well over a year.

It was okay to feel a bit nervous. Especially when he wasn't quite convinced that he'd made the right choice in coming here.

What if someone started questioning him and he said the wrong thing? Something that made them suspicious? He blew out an anxious breath and began searching the crowd of faces, seeking the woman he felt was, at least in part, somewhat responsible for his uneasiness. He found her squatted down to eye level in front of a small boy, conversing with him.

Garrett's stomach jumped into his throat at the touching scene. Inwardly he groaned. Why had he allowed this woman to penetrate her way into his life when it hadn't been his intention to do so? Was he slipping after all these months? Or was he simply getting tired of living life on the run?

Just as some thoughts were better left unsaid, other thoughts were better left alone, period. This was one of them. After all, he'd made himself a promise to protect his daughter at any cost, and he had known from the start that the costs would be many. Nothing had happened since he'd left San Francisco to change that. And while he might be tempted, he didn't have the time to wonder why some woman had gotten to him and some had not. He just needed to make sure she didn't do it again.

Glancing around, Whitney caught Garrett's gaze. Rising from her lowered position, she smiled at the boy and playfully ruffled his hair. When he scooted off in search of his friends, she walked over to Garrett and faced him. "I see you found the food."

Garrett glanced back at the table behind him. "Yeah. Our hostess insisted that Elsbeth and I have something to eat."

"That's our Sam," Whitney said knowingly. Shyly she took a step toward him. "Do you mind if I hold Elsbeth? I've been dying to."

Hesitating, Garrett looked down at his daughter and found her grinning at Whitney.

Damn, Garrett thought. It wasn't that he didn't feel he could trust this woman with his child. In fact, just the opposite was true. It was just that when she gazed at Elsbeth, there was such longing in the depths of her pale blue eyes that it worried him. What painful memory did his daughter stir to life in her? Whitney Sue Arceneaux might act as though her world was all peaches and cream, but Garrett's instincts were telling him that she was hurting like hell on the inside. She just pretended otherwise.

He watched as Whitney made a silly face for Elsbeth's benefit. Elsbeth pointed toward Whitney and babbled out her words as best she could for a sixteen-month-old. Garrett, not wanting to miss the opportunity to voice his own thoughts, interpreted his daughter's jumble and translated out loud for Whitney's benefit. "See the funny little clown, see her laughing."

Whitney knew the popular hit song from years ago that Garrett was quoting. And she also knew that the clown in that tune was anything but happy. Could he see through her act? Surely not. She'd become a master at the game of hiding her true feelings. Why, even as a child, she'd learned to accept her father's constant insults with a smile.

"Please," Whitney said, "could I hold her?"

Suddenly Garrett found that, for the moment at least, he couldn't have refused Whitney anything, not even if his life had depended on it. As a matter of fact, right now he would have done anything to bring back one of her bright smiles to her face. "Sure. She's all yours." He leaned toward Whitney, and Elsbeth slipped from his arms to hers.

Immediately one of the smiles Garrett had hoped to see again sprang to Whitney's face, causing every organ in his body to rally to the occasion, including his heart, which was pounding horrendously. "Now, that's better."

"What is?" she asked, tilting her head to one side.

"This," he replied, following the outline of her bottom lip with the tip of his finger. The very air around them seemed electrified.

Had he used a lightning rod to trace her lip he couldn't have charged her up more. Her insides sizzled to life. With her heart hammering against her chest, she took a step back. "Don't do that," she exclaimed curtly.

"What?" he drawled out. "This?" Again he traced her bottom lip from corner to corner, but this time his gaze poured into hers the entire time.

Whitney's breath evaporated from her body. Oh, for crying out loud, why was he so hell-bent on intimidating her? She could only suppose it was the grizzly in him. The wild beast that refused to conform to what polite society expected of him. To what *she* expected of him. Well, she'd already had her fill of grizzlies, thank you, world, just the same. "Please don't do that again," she said in a lowered voice.

Garrett frowned. He hadn't meant to upset her. But for some strange, uncontrollable reason, he had wanted to feel the softness of her full lips. For just one insane moment he'd felt a burning need to...to put his mouth where his finger had been. To run his tongue along the curve of her lip.

But now he was back in the real world, where the cold, hard facts of his life made that impossible. "I'm sorry. Look, would you like me to get you something to drink?" he asked, his voice an octave huskier than normal despite his best effort to appear nonchalant about what he'd just done to her and its gut-wrenching effect on him.

"Not really," Whitney replied, unable to meet his gaze. She hugged Elsbeth closer. The child's small arms encircled her neck. "You smell so good, sweetheart."

"Look," Garrett said, touching her arm, "I'm really sorry if I upset you. Frankly I don't know what came over me."

Elsbeth, unaware of the high-strung emotions ricocheting between her father and Whitney, chose that moment to pat Whitney on the cheek with her chubby little hand. "Mum...mum...mum..." she chimed.

Suddenly memories of another time and another little girl brought burning tears to Whitney's eyes. She immediately turned her head slightly so that Garrett wouldn't notice them. "Apology accepted."

A middle-aged gentleman with dark hair that was graying at the temples stepped up to Garrett. "So you're the new guy on the block, huh?" he said. "Well, I'm Tom Scallan and I live in the third house to the left." He gestured with his hand in that direction. "I've probably lived on this street longer than anyone here, so if you need to know anything, just ask me."

Still holding Elsbeth in her arms, Whitney took advantage of the interruption to stroll away from the two men. She needed the break from Garrett. For reasons she couldn't explain, the man got to her in ways she had promised herself that she would never let happen again.

Cradling Elsbeth in her arms, Whitney moved through the crowd, stopping momentarily when a friend asked her if she had eaten at the newly opened seafood restaurant on Airline Highway. She said she had and took a moment to rave about the delicious food, recommending both the stuffed mushrooms as an appetizer and grilled red snapper as an entrée.

Taking her time in crossing the backyard, Whitney waited until she felt she was quite a distance from where Garrett stood before she dared glance back. Tom Scallan was still speaking to him, but Whitney could tell that Garrett's full attention was devoted solely toward watching her carry his daughter farther and farther away from him. As their gazes locked, he narrowed his eyes and a shiver slid down Whitney's spine. The look he gave her wasn't exactly threatening, but there certainly was a warning in there somewhere, and Whitney instantly knew she had to make sure that she remained well within his sight as she mingled through the crowd. Otherwise, she felt certain, she would suddenly find herself confronted by one upset grizzly.

And it was said that the mother's instincts were the most powerful! Well, Garrett Wilson was certainly proving to be the exception to that rule.

He'd called himself a teddy bear. Just who was he trying to kid, anyway?

Whitney saw Samantha at the same time that her friend noticed her. Samantha hurried over.

"So what did you do to convince our mysterious new neighbor to come to the party?" Sam asked, smiling at Elsbeth as she spoke.

"I told him you thought he didn't have any friends," Whitney replied point-blank. She was still somewhat annoyed with Samantha for talking her into going over to Garrett's house, and for the moment she felt like getting even. She never should have listened to her.

"Oh, Whitney, you didn't! Did you?" Samantha asked, looking almost embarrassed that she'd said that about Garrett in the first place. "Tell me you didn't say that."

"Of course not," Whitney said. "Actually I was just being mean, and I apologize. But the next time you get some wild idea that involves me, I'm going to blow your cover and let it be known that it's all your doing, not mine."

"Well, he's here, isn't he? You must have said or done *something* right."

"I simply told him that everyone was curious about him. I said that his coming to the party might possibly put a stop to all the gossip about him. And then I told him that he'd probably have a good time. I guess he believed me."

"Well, have you noticed that he hasn't taken those gorgeous green eyes of his off you all night long?"

"As a matter of fact, I have."

"*Well?*"

"Well, what?" Whitney replied, quickly becoming exasperated with her friend. "I have his daughter in my arms."

"Well, is he or is he not your Knight in Shining Armor?"

Whitney almost choked on the absurdity of that question. "Good grief—no, Samantha. Now, will you please stop playing Little Miss Matchmaker? I'm not interested in the guy, and he certainly isn't interested in me."

"You're twenty-eight years old and you've never had a serious, romantic relationship with a man. Doesn't that worry you?"

"I don't give it a whole lot of thought. Apparently not as much as you do. I'm perfectly happy with my life." Whitney glanced at Elsbeth. "I only wish I still had Allison. I miss her."

"Oh, I know you do, honey," Samantha said, hugging Whitney to her.

"But I'm fine, Sam. Really I am. So please stop trying to pair me off with every eligible bachelor you meet. Okay?"

"Okay," Samantha said quietly. But Whitney wasn't fooled by her friend's subdued behavior. The two of them had had this conversation many times in the past, and knowing Samantha as she did, undoubtedly within a couple of months they would be having it again.

Whitney settled in a chair and placed Elsbeth in her lap. The child seemed to be enjoying all the attention she was receiving. But when one of the male guests standing near them spoke in a loud, robust voice, she leaned her small frame against Whitney; Whitney automatically tightened her arms around the child.

"It's okay, honey," Whitney whispered reassuringly. "He's really a nice man. Besides, I'm here and I won't let anything happen to you." Hoping to comfort her, Whitney rocked back and forth in her seat.

Elsbeth stuck her thumb in her mouth and rested her head back against Whitney's breasts, shutting her eyes.

It took Whitney a couple of minutes to realize that Elsbeth had fallen asleep. She gazed down at the exhausted baby in her arms and for a fraction of a second pictured another time and another child, one with strawberry blond hair and pale blue eyes. How often had she rocked Allison to sleep? She bent to kiss the child's forehead, and it was only when her lips touched Elsbeth's baby-soft skin that she awakened from her daze and once again recognized that the mop of dark brown curls atop the child's head belonged to Elsbeth, and not to Allison. She kissed Elsbeth's forehead once more, as though, now fully aware of whom she held, she wanted to give the little girl her own special kiss. The child deserved that much. Actually she deserved so much more. Certainly more than Whitney could ever give her. For several pain-filled moments, Whitney regretted that she had already given away all the love she had to give.

Mentally far away from the action and noise around her, Whitney had the sudden urge to hum Elsbeth the same lullaby she'd sung so many times to Allison.

Just then a shadow fell upon her, and Whitney glanced up to see that Garrett had finally found her small corner hideaway. But instead of his usual grizzly glare, this time he was actually smiling at her. "She asleep?" he asked, squatting down by Elsbeth's feet. "I guess I should have known she'd do this. She woke up early this morning and only took about a thirty-minute nap after lunch."

Giving Garrett a poignant smile, Whitney ran gentle fingers through the silky texture of Elsbeth's hair. "She's just a baby, you know. We can't expect her to keep up with the rest of us."

"I don't," Garrett replied, gently rubbing the backside of his index finger up and down Elsbeth's soft cheek. Strangely he found he had to restrain himself from immediately doing the same against Whitney's. "They sure have a way of getting to you, though, don't they?"

Oh, God, Whitney thought. Garrett had no earthly idea what his words were doing to her.

"Yes, they do," Whitney replied as hot tears sprang into her eyes, despite her best efforts to prevent them. She lowered her head. One warm tear dropped on Elsbeth.

"Hey, honey, look, I'm sorry," Garrett said, placing his fingers under her chin and forcing her to look into his eyes. Then he used those same big fingers to wipe away a single tear that slid down her cheek.

"Can I help?" Garrett asked, knowing full well that getting involved with her personal life was the last thing he needed. But how could he possibly listen to his common sense when Whitney Sue Arceneaux looked as though she was totally alone in this world and needed a friend to talk to?

Whitney shook her head. "There's nothing anyone can do. Please, I'm all right, really I am."

"Well, I'm ready to see a smile, if you don't mind. Look, nothing can be that bad, now can it?"

"You're right," Whitney replied with a shake of her head. Good grief. What insane reason did she have for acting like this—and at a party, no less?

She had two. Allison. And now little Elsbeth.

Well, maybe she had three. Because Garrett was in there somewhere; she just wasn't exactly sure where he fit in.

Now wasn't *that* proof enough that she was losing her grip on things?

"Isn't this supposed to be a party?" Whitney asked brightly, determined to change the subject. "And not only that, but I'm supposed to be helping out with the other guests." She attempted to rise to her feet, but the low chair she sat in and Elsbeth's extra weight was too much for her.

"Let me have Elsbeth," Garrett said.

"No, that's all right," Whitney said, once again trying to stand. This time she succeeded . . . and found herself standing face-to-face with Garrett.

"You can't very well carry Elsbeth around all night," Garrett pointed out gently.

"But..." Whitney looked down at the sleeping child. "I..."

"Whitney?"

"Of course," she said, releasing the child to him. "She's your daughter."

Garrett placed Elsbeth so that her head rested on his shoulder. "The kid's had all she can take for one day."

"Actually so have I," Whitney said.

"So you're leaving, too?" Garrett asked.

"Yes, I think I will," Whitney replied, suddenly wanting to get to the safety of her home very badly. "That is, if Sam doesn't still need my help."

"I'll wait for you."

"Oh, but that's not necessary—"

"I'm sure it isn't, but I'll wait, anyway." Garrett ended her protest quickly.

"Well, all right," Whitney said reluctantly, going off to find their hostess.

Moments later Whitney strolled toward her house with Garrett following only a few steps behind. The balmy, star-studded night held just a hint of a warm summer breeze.

Normally she would have entered her house from the rear, which was well lit for just such an occasion, but because her front-porch light was on and due to the fact that Garrett was in such close pursuit, Whitney chose the front entrance instead. She'd hoped she could deter Garrett from following her up the steps, but she was wrong. He didn't stop until they reached her door.

Whitney fumbled with her keys until she finally found the correct one and was able to slip it into the lock. She pushed open the door and stepped inside. "Thanks for walking me home," she said, turning to face him. "I know you must be in a hurry to get Elsbeth to bed."

"Well, actually..."

"Yes?" Whitney said, wondering what he could possibly want. Predators seldom hesitated before attacking. Was this her last chance to escape?

"Two sugars and one cream was more what I had in mind."

"What?"

"In my coffee. I like it with two sugars and one cream."

"Coffee?"

"Uh-huh."

"You want me to make coffee for you?"

He grinned, and Whitney's stomach turned to apple butter right there in the doorway. "Good girl," he said, sounding for all the world as if he was laughing at her. "Now you're catching on."

"Right," Whitney replied sorely.

Okay, world, she told herself, it was time she got back in control here. "I don't have instant coffee, just dark roast. You probably won't like it."

"Sounds good to me."

"It's one hundred percent caffeine."

"Great."

Whitney walked through the parlor and into the kitchen. "Two sugars and one cream," she mumbled out loud.

"That'll do it," Garrett replied, keeping in step just behind her.

Whitney shrugged as a shiver ran down the length of her. "Well, suit yourself. But don't blame me if you're up half the night."

He gave a humorless laugh. "I'll probably be up half the night, anyway, Whitney, but I can assure you that your coffee won't have a thing to do with it."

She looked back over her shoulder with the intention of asking him what he meant. But instead their gazes met, and from the sizzling intensity in his, Whitney instantly realized that she already knew the answer to her question, heaven help her. And then she went hot all over.

Chapter Four

Willing herself under control, Whitney clicked on the electric coffeemaker located near her stove. "Would you like to place Elsbeth on the sofa while you're having your coffee?" she offered.

"Yeah," Garrett said. "That's a good idea."

Whitney led the way into the living room. She watched as Garrett carefully placed Elsbeth on the blue plaid couch and then removed the child's small white sneakers from her feet.

Unconsciously intent on Garrett's every move, Whitney didn't notice the sad smile that touched her lips, put there by the ever-represent memory of her niece and her growing fondness for this motherless child. "Does her mama ever see her?" she heard herself asking.

Garrett's movements came to an abrupt halt, but he didn't glance up at her as he spoke. "No. My ex-wife lives in another state."

"I see," Whitney replied, feeling even sadder at the realization that Elsbeth's mother probably missed her as much as Whitney missed Allison. But if Garrett didn't want to elaborate on why the woman didn't come to visit her little girl, she wasn't going to ask. Instead, she gazed down at the sleeping child. "Don't you think we'd better stay in here with her? She could tumble off, you know."

Garrett continued to gaze down at his daughter. "I doubt if she'll even move, but you're right. I should keep an eye on her."

"I'll bring the coffee in here."

"You sure it's no trouble?"

Now he was worrying about trouble. Well, it was too late for that. She had a sneaky feeling they were both sliding toward more trouble than either of them could possibly imagine at the moment. "Of course not. I'll be just a minute."

In the kitchen Whitney poured the hot brew into two coffee mugs and then stirred two teaspoons of sugar and one teaspoon of cream into Garrett's. Next she prepared her own.

It was hard to believe that only a few short hours ago, Garrett Wilson wouldn't even give her a greeting from across the street. Now she couldn't seem to get rid of him.

Nor did she want to, exactly—and that alone should have warned her it was past time to say good night, but she merely walked back out to where he sat on the sofa next to Elsbeth, placed the mugs of coffee on the table in front of him and then sat down in a blue tufted chair.

Garrett lifted his mug and took a sip. "That sure hits the spot."

"Yes, it does," Whitney said, adding to their idle conversation. But then what else was there for them to do besides make small talk?

The sudden image of her and Garrett in her bed, making wild, passionate love did a slow stroll across her mind. Having chosen that exact moment to take her first swallow of coffee, Whitney, startled by the picture, nearly strangled on the hot liquid as it burned a path down her throat.

Immediately she knew that that particular injury was probably just for starters. No doubt her entire mouth was scorched as a result—and that was from the hot coffee. But the other burning sensation she felt in yet another part of her body was caused, she knew, by the sultry, wanton vision she'd had of herself and Garrett.

Breathing deeply, she quietly reminded herself that she simply had to regain control of her back-stabbing imagination and not let it rule her in that way again. At least the painful swallow of hot coffee had purged the ridiculous thought of them making love from her mind.

Or had it?

Yes, darn it, it had, she told herself while shaking her head to clear it. Still, the nagging, heart-stopping image persisted. His naked, giving body was magnificent. In her imaginings he wasn't at all what she thought a grizzly would be....

Garrett sat back in his seat. "May I ask you something?"

Whitney blinked twice. "Yes, I suppose so," she replied, feeling a blush rush to her face. She felt shaken to the core.

"I probably shouldn't ask this. It's rather personal—and probably none of my business."

"Oh?" Whitney asked, widening her eyes a fraction of an inch wider than normal, trying to look innocent. *Oh, Lord, had he read her thoughts?*

"Earlier, when we were at the barbecue, you looked so unhappy. I thought you might need to talk about it with someone."

"I don't know what you mean," Whitney said too quickly. With shaking hands, she placed her mug on the table in front of her. All of her defensive mechanisms sprang to life.

"Look, Whitney, you didn't fool me for a minute. And I doubt if you fooled anyone else, either. Something was obviously bothering you at the party."

"Well, you are correct about one thing," Whitney said, rising to her feet. "My moods aren't any of your business."

Garrett stood, too. "Hey," he said, placing his hand on her arm to prevent her from moving farther away. "I just thought you might need a friend, that's all."

Great, Whitney thought. Just what she needed. A sympathetic grizzly. "It's not at all what you think," Whitney said, pulling free from his grasp and taking a step back in order to put some distance between them.

"Actually I don't know what to think about you. One minute you're the bubbly neighbor from across the street. Then, in the next minute, you're one sad lady," Garrett said, wondering if he was totally losing his mind for wanting to get involved with her and her problems. Ignoring his common sense, he reached out and touched one corner of her mouth. "Smile, honey. Nothing can be that bad."

"I assure you, it's not," Whitney said, realizing she needed to get this man—this stranger—out of her house before she broke down in front of him. No man would ever see her in such a state again. Not ever.

"Well, if you need to talk about—"

"I don't," she replied tersely, cutting him off.

"Okay. I just wanted to help if I could."

"Well, you can't."

"So, you're admitting you need—"

"I'm not admitting anything."

"Okay. I can see when I'm getting nowhere," Garrett said, shaking his head. "But if you should change your mind—"

"I won't."

"Fine, then," he said abruptly. He turned away from her and gathered up Elsbeth from the sofa. "Thanks for the coffee."

"Don't mention it," Whitney said with a tight smile on her lips. She held the door open for him and watched as he walked across the street with his daughter in his arms.

Whitney had hoped for a full eight hours of sleep. But after rising the next morning at seven o'clock, she realized she had lain awake for most of the night, longing for Allison and wishing that sweet little Elsbeth had a mother who would care for her in a way the little girl deserved. Because if that had been the case, Whitney knew she would have had nothing to fear. But as it was, she felt she was in danger of losing her already broken heart to another tiny urchin with big, round, innocent eyes. Simply put, the child had a way of tugging at her heartstrings. Not to mention, Whitney thought, the way a mere glance from the child's father could mesmerize her. But what if she came to care for Garrett in the same way she had cared for her brother-in-law? And what if he, like her brother-in-law, tossed her feelings aside?

Taking a deep breath, she reaffirmed the promise she had made to herself. From now on, she would stay as far away as she could from Garrett Wilson and his motherless child. It was for her own good.

Dressing in a peach-colored sundress, and just as she often did around eight o'clock on Sunday mornings, Whitney went to meet Samantha and Jim, who were on their patio having coffee. Immediately Samantha began questioning her.

"So now that it's just the three of us," her friend said, lifting her perfectly groomed eyebrows, "let's have the truth. Just why did you and our new elusive neighbor leave the party last night?" By this time Samantha had a smile on her face that told Whitney Sam thought she already knew the answer.

Jim Erwin had just sat down in one of the four wrought-iron straight-back chairs surrounding a large circular patio table. A big yellow umbrella overhead shaded him from the bright morning sun. "Just so you know, Whitney," he cut in, "it doesn't really matter what you say. Sam has already formed her own opinion on the matter."

Whitney smiled as she took a seat next to him. "So you saw that look, too, huh?"

"What look?" Samantha asked, placing her hands on her hips.

Whitney's grin widened. "You know. That look you get when you refuse to listen to reason and form your own opinion about something."

"Why, that's not true," Samantha denied indignantly. But then she broke into a smile. "Well…maybe I do that sometimes."

Whitney and Jim both laughed out loud. "Only *sometimes,* honey?" he asked.

"Why, James Erwin, you make me sound like I'm a busybody."

"Well, you are, puddin'. But I love you, anyway."

"Well, I love you, too. So I'll forgive you," Samantha replied, wrinkling her nose at her husband. "And Whitney's my best friend, so I'll forgive her, as well. Besides, I know that both of you would be lost without me."

"It's kind of you to forgive us," Whitney said with a chuckle.

"Well, it's the least I can do. I know it's too early in the morning for Jim, and you're simply not thinking straight. Of course, I know why."

Shaking her head, Whitney sighed. "There you go again. Making all kinds of assumptions."

"Well, my goodness, what else can I do? You haven't told me a thing about this guy."

"There isn't anything to tell. Besides, you haven't exactly given me a chance."

Pouring herself another cup of coffee, Samantha quickly plopped back down in her chair, crossed one leg over the other and then smiled at her friend. "Okay, so here's your chance."

In spite of the mild depression she had suffered earlier that morning, Whitney was now feeling better. But then Samantha and Jim always made her feel good about things. They were so much in love with each other and with life that it was catching. For the first six months after Allison had been taken away from her, they had been her salvation.

Suddenly Samantha stood and hurried to the corner of the patio that was nearest the front lawn. "Well, looky here, you two." She pointed toward the front. "Look who's driving away."

Neither Whitney nor Jim moved, though for just a moment Whitney was tempted to jump to her feet. Instead, she slowly shook her head. "Sam, what is it about this guy that makes you think he's so perfect for me?"

The telephone started ringing and Jim rose and hurried inside to answer it. Sam waited until Jim had gone, and then she said, "Well, I know how much you miss Allison and I thought maybe his daughter—"

"Now, hold on," Whitney exclaimed. "First off, you know that no child is ever going to replace Allison. Elsbeth is precious, but she's not Allison. And she's also none of my concern and I plan to keep it that way."

Samantha didn't back down. "There's something that I never realized until last night. It wasn't just Allison that broke your heart, was it? There was more to it than that." Samantha waited for Whitney to answer, but she didn't.

"Honey, please don't tell me you actually fell for that jerk of a brother-in-law you had."

Again Whitney chose not to answer.

Samantha sighed. "Well, at least that finally explains a lot of things. No wonder you fell completely apart when he took off with Allison—and his new girl-friend."

"But I'm back together now. And I owe the thanks to both you and Jim for that—I don't know what I would have done without ya'll. Besides, what happened to me was my own fault, anyway. Jeff never made me any promises."

"No. But he certainly didn't mind taking advantage of your vulnerability during a very sad time in your life, now did he?" Sam replied. "He lost his wife when Lisa was killed, but you lost your sister and Allison lost her mother. He took your pain and used it to his own advantage. Don't forget that.''

"But that's beside the point," Whitney said quietly. "*I* should have known better. I didn't even like the way he treated Lisa before she died. But I somehow convinced myself that his losing her so tragically had changed him. Had made him finally see the true-blue things that are really important in life. I guess I was wrong.''

"Aw, honey, I'm sorry," Samantha said. "I should have realized your feelings long before now. I could have helped you get through it better. I just didn't know.''

Placing her empty cup on the wrought-iron table, Whitney rose from her chair, hurried over to where Samantha stood and gave her a hug. "I didn't want you to. I didn't want anyone to know I'd been such a fool.''

Samantha hugged Whitney back tightly.

"Hey," Jim said as he returned, his grin as bright as the morning sunshine. "I think I deserve a little of that, too.''

Not to be outdone, both women walked over and gave him a hug, only Samantha topped hers with a kiss. When she was finished, she looked over at Whitney. "I still say that guy's worth a try. Even Jim thinks he's kind of mysterious. Don't you, honey?''

"You don't give up, do you?" Whitney asked, a lighthearted note of exasperation in her voice.

"Whitney, if you don't mind, I think I'll answer that question for you," Jim replied. He looked over at his wife and shook his head in mock seriousness. "Not ever.''

Acting as though her feelings were hurt, Samantha pushed out her bottom lip. "Looks like I won't have any choice this time, though. Whitney refuses to take my advice, even though I'm convinced it's for her own good."

"I know you think it is, Sam, and that's why I can't get angry with you. But please, I'm a grown woman. I need to make my own choices."

"Well," Samantha replied, "you certainly didn't hesitate in telling me I should marry Jim."

"And aren't you glad you took my advice?"

Samantha relented and smiled, plopping down in her husband's lap. "Only during every single moment of my life. So maybe you should take my advice." She shrugged. "Who knows what might happen?"

Whitney ignored Sam's last comment. Turning in the direction of her house, she began walking away even as she spoke. "I've got to get going. I'm taking my mother to church at eleven and then to Damon's for Sunday brunch."

"Say hi for us, will you? Oh—and while you're at it, have an extra dessert on me," Samantha said.

Whitney patted the sides of her hips and laughed. "Not on your life."

Garrett drove to the local supermarket in a tiff with himself. He couldn't believe he'd run out of clean diapers for Elsbeth. What kind of father ran out of diapers for his own kid?

A preoccupied one.

What in the world was happening to him? Hadn't he gone to the store just yesterday?

Maybe it was time he listened to his gut feelings and got the hell out of Dodge while he still had some measure of brain activity left.

His sixth sense was seldom wrong. Even in the beginning of his relationship with his ex-wife, something had told him that she was going to be big trouble. Two years later he'd had that same gut feeling, only to discover that he'd accidentally spoiled what had been an attempt by his ex-in-laws to kidnap Elsbeth. That was the reason he felt he had to get her away from them.

And now that same *something* was trying to warn him again. Whitney Sue Arceneaux could easily mess up his plans but good. And yet, heaven help him, he couldn't stop thinking about her. To kiss her full mouth would be to have a small taste of heaven.

Garrett groaned as heat spread through him. Damn. Obviously his real problem was that he'd been without a woman for too long.

Yeah, that was it, he assured himself.

Besides, neither his nor Whitney Arceneaux's happiness was what he needed to be concerned about. Only Elsbeth's welfare mattered. And he wasn't going to allow himself to lose perspective on that.

He arrived at the supermarket and took Elsbeth inside with him. A few minutes later he'd collected all the items he needed, checked them out and was heading back home.

As he was opening the front door, his telephone was ringing. From old habit he rushed to answer it. But just before picking up the receiver, he hesitated. Not many people had his number—only his brother, his employer and the woman who baby-sat Elsbeth while he worked.

He took a deep breath and cautiously lifted the receiver. "Hello?"

"Mr. Wilson?" a female voice said.

"Who is this?" Garrett immediately asked.

"It's Gloria Ortego, Mr. Wilson. And I'm afraid I have some bad news for you."

Garrett's gut knotted up. He feared he already knew what his baby-sitter had to say. More than likely, she had just received a visit or a call from one of his ex-in-laws' hired detectives. Hadn't he known that staying in one place for very long was a dumb thing for him to try to do?

Damn it, he'd known what would happen. But his desire to give Elsbeth just a taste of what normal living was like had convinced him to give it a try. He'd hoped that maybe, in the years to come, these few months of stability would have some profound effect on her life. That maybe somewhere in her innocent mind, Elsbeth would store away the memory and keep it for when she needed it most. For the time, should it ever happen, that he couldn't be there for her anymore.

God, he couldn't bear the thought of that.

He cleared his throat and willed himself to remain in control. "What is it, Mrs. Ortego?"

Whitney was busy working on her two new accounts. Having made the decision to quit her full-time job with a local accounting firm soon after Lisa was killed, she still hadn't any regrets about starting her own business at home. It had given her the time she had needed in order to grieve her sister's death and to care for the small baby she'd left behind.

But time had yet to completely heal all her wounds, and oftentimes Whitney wondered if it ever would.

Around seven she ate a light supper, then showered and wrapped her hair in a towel to keep it damp while she watched her favorite Sunday program on television. She would blow her hair dry after the show was over. She quickly applied a thin application of the new mud facial she'd purchased at the supermarket the day before and set the timer to remind her when it would be necessary to remove it. Now that caring for Allison was no longer a part of her life, this was a Sunday-night ritual that she seldom had reason to change.

As she headed into the living room, she saw that it had begun to drizzle outside, which kind of surprised her because the weatherman hadn't said it was going to rain today. But then, everyone knew that south Louisiana's weather was unpredictable. The warm waters of the Gulf of Mexico, which weren't that far away, were a breeding ground for sudden changes.

After sitting on the sofa and using the remote control to flick on the television, Whitney adjusted her mid-length terry-cloth bathrobe so she would be more comfortable. Feeling a tightening sensation on her face from the facial, she patted her cheeks lightly as she glanced at herself in the mirror hanging on a nearby wall. She grimaced. Even her mouth looked as though it was being molded into a pucker. Heavens, she looked like the creature from the Black Lagoon.

The knock at her door sounded first, then the timer went off a half second later. Darn, just when her program was getting started.

Not sure in which direction to go first, she decided to answer the knock. "Yes? Who is it?" Whitney asked through the closed door, not willing to confront just anyone with the way she looked.

"It's me, Garrett Wilson, your neighbor from across the street."

Garrett!

Oh, God. He couldn't see her like this. Even Godzilla didn't need to see her looking like this.

"Well, you'll just have to wait for a minute before I can open the door."

Just then there was a loud crack of thunder, and Whitney heard a child scream.

"Could you make it fast?" Garrett yelled. "Elsbeth's frightened out of her mind out here."

Jerking open the door, Whitney exclaimed, "Oh—all right! Come in."

"Thanks," Garrett said, barreling in with his daughter in tow. "Man, that storm came up fast—"

At that moment he looked over at Whitney, and his face went blank. "My God, what have you done to yourself?"

"Oh!" Whitney exclaimed, placing the palms of her hands over her cheeks. "I forgot." Embarrassed, she whirled around and ran down the hall. "I'll be back in a minute."

Slamming the bathroom door behind her, Whitney glanced at herself in the mirror over the lavatory one last time and cringed. Good grief! No wonder Garrett was so shocked by her appearance. She looked like a dried-up prune. She began splashing cool water on her face to soften the hardening mud. Then she tore away the white towel wrapped around her head and began combing the tangles from her damp hair, a task not easily accomplished.

Why me? she thought.

Three minutes later she emerged from the bathroom, face cleaned, hair combed and hot tempered. Just who in the world did Garrett Wilson think he was, barging in on her and then making her feel guilty for scaring the dickens out of him? *What had she done to herself, indeed!*

Whitney walked back into the living room and found Garrett still standing in the same spot. Ignoring him—never mind that he had on a blue T-shirt that emphasized his lean, muscled chest and a pair of worn jeans that hugged his narrow hips and demanded that she follow their cut down to his shoes—she smiled at Elsbeth. "Hi, sweetie."

The child's face lit up with recognition and she threw her arms out toward Whitney, surprising both Whitney and her father.

"Well, come here," Whitney said, her voice quickly thickening with emotion. Elsbeth slipped from Garrett's arms to hers.

Whitney wiped away Elsbeth's tears while coaxing her in a soothing voice. "There's nothing to be afraid of, sweetie. It's just the silly wind outside. You're safe in here with us." Whitney hugged the child's sturdy little body to her own.

"You're really good with kids, do you know that?" Garrett asked, observing her closely. "I noticed that at the party last night."

"Umm . . . I've had a bit of practice," she replied distractedly, burying her nose in Elsbeth's sweet-smelling hair and inhaling deeply.

Garrett glanced over at the color portrait of Allison, which hung on the wall nearby. "Who's the kid?" he asked.

Without looking in that direction, she replied, "My niece."

"Oh. I thought she might have been yours."

"I thought of her as mine," Whitney replied. "I took care of her for a long time after my sister was killed."

"I'm sorry about your sister."

"Yes. It was tragic—for all of us."

"Do you still baby-sit your niece?"

"I didn't just baby-sit her," Whitney said, piqued that no one truly understood the way she felt about Allison. But she knew she was being unfair. How could he possibly know? "Allison was like my own."

"Care to explain that?"

"No."

"Maybe you'd feel better if you did."

"I doubt that," Whitney replied, again deliberately giving Elsbeth her full attention. She made a funny face so that the child would smile.

Garrett frowned. Trying to continue a conversation with Whitney was like trying to convince himself that he needed to eat raw oysters. He could never quite do it. "Look, I've got a real problem and I was hoping you could help me with it."

Whitney shrugged. "What kind of problem?"

"I know this is sudden and all, but...well...the lady who baby-sits for Elsbeth called today to say her brother's had a massive heart attack and that she has to leave for Little Rock, Arkansas, immediately."

"I'm sorry to hear that," Whitney replied. "When will she be back?"

"She doesn't know. Her sister-in-law is handicapped and may need some help caring for him."

"I see." An unexpected anxiety began to grow in Whitney. Surely he wasn't going to ask her to... to...

"Look, the reason I came over here is because... well, I mean... I was wondering if you would consider taking over the job of baby-sitting Elsbeth until Mrs. Ortego returns."

Whitney felt breathless. *Not again.* "I can't do that."

"But last night I thought I overheard you tell a friend that you've had plenty of free time lately."

"Well, I did say that," Whitney continued defensively. "But I've just added two new clients and I expect to be quite busy from now on."

"It shouldn't be for more than a day or two."

"Or a week or two," Whitney argued back.

Garrett shrugged. "Yeah. I guess it could be that long. I really have no way of knowing."

Whitney's gut knotted up. "Look, there are plenty of day-care centers. I'm sure one of them—"

"I can't just turn her care over to complete strangers. I felt she was safe with Mrs. Ortego. The woman was recommended to me by a fellow employee."

"But I'm a stranger to you, too," Whitney exclaimed.

He stared at her with those mesmerizing green eyes of his. "Yes, but I feel I know you well enough to leave Elsbeth in your care. Call it a sixth sense, whatever, but I know she'd be safe with you. And the bottom line is," he continued, drawing in a deep breath, "tomorrow I'm starting a new job and I'd sure hate to miss my first day. I don't think the boss would like it one bit. As a matter of fact, he might very well decide that he doesn't need my help, after all. Surely you can understand my predicament."

She did. But his problems weren't hers. "Other people use day-care centers. Why can't you?" Whitney asked.

"I have my reasons," Garrett said tightly.

"Well, would you mind expressing them to me so I can better understand why you seem so strongly against them?"

"I'm not against them. But I can't explain," he replied, those intense green eyes boring into hers. Whitney found she was unable to look away. "Besides, it wouldn't change anything if I did. If you can't do it, then you can't do it."

What was his problem, for heaven's sake? And what in the world was hers? Whitney wondered. Why was she having such mixed feelings about turning him down? She hugged Elsbeth tighter to herself. This child wasn't her concern, and her father had no right asking for her to be.

God! How could something like this be happening to her again?

"I can't," Whitney said in a voice barely above a whisper. She felt as though she might burst into tears and tried hard to keep them from gathering in her eyes. "I just . . . can't."

"Look, I understand," he said abruptly, reaching for his daughter. Whitney moved the child from his reach. "Can't I hold her just a moment more?"

Placing his big hands on his hips, Garrett gazed down at her. Ignoring her request, his jaw hardened. "I realize I shouldn't have asked this of you in the first place. It's not your problem. I'll try to work something else out. Now, would you please let me have my daughter back?"

When he lifted Elsbeth from Whitney's arms, it felt as though he had ripped away some vital part of her body.

But her answer was still no.

No. No. *No.*

Garrett opened the door to leave, and the storm tore it from his grasp and crashed it against the house. The abrupt noise, in combination with the wind and rain outdoors, caused Elsbeth to start crying again.

Grabbing hold of Garrett's arm to prevent him from walking out, Whitney said quietly, "You can't take her home in this weather. She'll be hysterical by the time you get there."

Garrett held Elsbeth close to him, comforting her. Whitney shut the door and attempted to help him calm her.

It was then she realized that she and Garrett had moved near enough to each other that he could have easily wrapped her in his embrace, too. And for just one fleeting moment, she desperately wished he would. She glanced up and saw him looking at her through watchful, almost brooding eyes.

Whitney felt her heart pounding. "How long did you say your baby-sitter will be gone?"

"It's hard to say. A day or two. Maybe more."

"Well," she said, staring into his hypnotic gaze, "Maybe . . . I mean . . . perhaps I *could* help you out for a day or two."

"It's okay, Whitney. I shouldn't have asked it of you in the first place," Garrett said, his intense gaze still leveled on her.

"But I really would like to help out. Besides, I hate to see Elsbeth placed with total strangers. Especially with it being for such a short period of time, and all. I'm sure I can manage for a few days."

Garrett moved closer to her. "Are you sure about this?"

"Positive," Whitney replied, her heart pounding in her ears.

She gazed up into his face and saw when a faint grin touched his lips. Then he leaned toward her, and she knew without a doubt that he was going to kiss her.

She closed her eyes, and a moment later his warm lips touched hers in a sweet, feather-light union. Then he pulled away.

It wasn't enough of him. She wanted more.

"Thanks, Whitney," he said, his voice sounding deep and rich. Her eyes flickered open. "I'll owe you one."

If the truth be known, she would have preferred that he owe her two—or even three—more like the one he'd just given her. "Don't mention it," she replied, wondering in what direction her good sense had ventured off to and whether or not the rest of her would follow suit.

So much, she thought to herself, for her big, tough decision not to get involved in Garrett Wilson's life.

Chapter Five

With her eyes still watery with tears, Elsbeth stuck her thumb in her mouth and then laid her dark head on her father's shoulder. Her other arm encircled the back of his neck.

"She looks tired," Whitney said, a frown etching its way across her forehead as she smoothed back the child's damp curls.

"And hungry," Garrett added, gazing down at his daughter. "We haven't had our supper yet."

"Well, for goodness' sakes," Whitney exclaimed. "She must be starving by now. It's after eight."

"We always eat late," Garrett replied defensively. He shifted his weight from one foot to the other and wondered who in the world had given this woman the right to chastise him. Hell, he was doing the best he could. Was it his fault that he wasn't meeting her standard when it came to being a perfect father? He sure as hell didn't think so. "Her diaper probably needs changing, too."

From the disgruntled look on his neighbor's face, Garrett quickly decided that his last statement had just plunged him into deeper trouble. The woman was looking at him in a way that made him feel as though he were doing a lousy job at being a parent. Like he was some kind of animal. What had she called him? A grizzly? Yeah, that was it. She was making him feel as if he were nothing more than a mean old grizzly.

"Well, I hadn't exactly planned on staying for more than a couple of minutes," he said, angry with himself for wanting to justify his actions. After all, it wasn't actually any of her business, now was it? At least, not yet. Her baby-sitting services didn't start until eight o'clock tomorrow morning. Until then *he* was in charge of Elsbeth—not her. "And silly me," he went on with a hand gesture to his forehead that suggested he had no brains at all, "as of yet I haven't gotten in the habit of carrying around a spare diaper in my back pocket."

"Well, you should," Whitney said, taking control of the situation by removing Elsbeth from his arms as if she had every given right to. "Thank goodness I still have a half-empty box of disposable diapers in the bathroom closet." Cradling Elsbeth, she started toward the room. "Allison wasn't wearing diapers anymore but—"

With a start Whitney realized where her thoughts had automatically flown. Taking a deep breath, she paused and waited for the tightness in her chest to ease. God, but it hurt when bittersweet memories of Allison flooded her mind like this.

"Anyway, I never throw anything away, so I'm sure they're still in the closet somewhere. I just hope they fit Elsbeth," she said, determined to keep her thoughts in the present. Remembering the many times she had changed Allison's diapers and powdered her small bottom with clean-smelling talc wasn't going to help her any at this point. "We wouldn't want someone as sugar sweet as Elsbeth developing a diaper rash, now would we?" she said in a tone of voice that clearly stated that she was speaking more to the child she carried in her arms than to the man who followed close behind.

Whitney opened the bathroom closet and saw the box of diapers on the top shelf. Once she'd considered throwing them away; there certainly hadn't been a need to keep them. But for some reason she could never quite convince herself to pitch them out.

Now she was glad. Glad that the diapers would be put to good use. Glad that she could help this motherless child, even if it was just in this small way. And yes, as hard as it was for her to admit it, glad that Garrett had chosen her to care for his daughter for the next few days. He was right about one thing. She would do everything in her power to see to it that Elsbeth was kept safe and sound.

Whitney walked into her bedroom, placed Elsbeth on her bed and, with the confidence that only experience could bring, changed her diaper. Garrett stood nearby, his long fingers tucked into the front pockets of his jeans, and watched. "I guess she should be potty trained by now," he said. "But I haven't done anything about that yet."

Shrugging, Whitney made a comical face at Elsbeth. The child grinned, and Whitney tickled her on the stomach. "Some people are really big on having their babies trained at an early age. Personally I'm a bit old-fashioned. As far as I'm concerned, around two years old is soon enough."

"Then you don't think it's terrible of me to have put it off for so long?" He stepped up next to Whitney, and their arms touched.

A jolt of electricity shot through her. "N-no," she stammered, trying to get the rest of her body to catch up with her racing heart. She didn't dare look at him. "I think you're doing the right thing by not rushing her."

"You're kidding," he exclaimed. "Do you mean to tell me that you actually think I'm doing something right for a change?"

She gave him a sharp glance. "I never said you did anything wrong."

"But you've implied it," Garrett argued, leveling those intense green eyes of his on her face. Inwardly she moaned. She always felt hot—volatile—when he did that. "Several times, as a matter of fact."

Momentarily ignored by the two adults standing over her, Elsbeth grew impatient for attention, rolled onto her side and began a fast-pace crawl toward the queen-size headboard. She grabbed hold of something that was tucked under one of the two pillows and pulled it from its hiding place.

Whitney's whole body froze into place. The some-thing-or-other was the bra she'd wanted to wear today but hadn't because she couldn't find where she'd placed the darn thing when she'd stopped dressing for a mo-ment to answer the telephone. But thanks to Elsbeth, she now realized where she'd unconsciously placed her favorite bra. Hip-hip-hooray! Wave the banner.

Actually Elsbeth was already in the process of doing just that. Only the banner she waved was no flag. It was Whitney's peach-colored, lace-trimmed bra. Rolling onto her back, the child put her chubby leg through the opening of one strap.

Garrett sprang into action. "Come here, Lissy," he said, swerving his long legs around the corner of Whitney's bed to stop his daughter's antics. Elsbeth giggled when Garrett caught her by the foot and playfully pulled her to him. Whitney's bra came right along with her.

Garrett gathered up Elsbeth, who was more than willing to share her new find with her father. "Da-da," she exclaimed, giggling as she tried dangling the bra over her face. "Goo' girl."

Garrett laughed as he untangled the undergarment from her leg and held it out to Whitney. "Rough night?"

"Oh, for heaven's sakes!"

As soon as she yanked it from his grasp, he grinned and began a slow, deliberate examination of her room, which for some unexplained reason truly unnerved that part of herself that still had a fair amount of feeling left. But what made matters worse, he looked as though he knew of her total discomfort and couldn't have cared less. Well, by golly, just how would he have liked it if his daughter had been waving around his jockstrap as if it were an international goodwill flag or something? She certainly wouldn't have worn a smirky I'm-the-cat-that-just-ate-the-mouse look on her face, Whitney thought. *She* had more tact than that.

"So," he finally said in a deep-timbred voice, "this is where you sleep, huh?"

No, the Wicked Witch of the West sleeps here.

"This is my room, all right," Whitney replied with a nervous shake of her head. Surreptitiously placing the bra inside her top drawer, she tucked her fingertips into the pockets of her robe and turned back to face Garrett.

Still gazing around, Garrett said, "It looks like a woman's room. Smells like one, too."

"Oh?" Whitney replied, taking two quick sniffs. What had he meant by that? She didn't smell anything different. "How does it smell to you?"

"Pretty."

"Pretty," she repeated to herself as she took another whiff. Now what, to his way of thinking, qualified a smell as being pretty?

Suddenly she became self-conscious of all the paraphernalia she had either placed upon her provincial furnishings or tossed carelessly across a white wicker rocker in one corner of the room. The black lace bra and matching panty laid out on the wicker seat were what she had intended on wearing a couple of days ago under a black dress. But at the last minute she'd changed her mind and worn something else.

Now it seemed she would live to regret not putting away those darn undergarments as she'd intended. She peeked at Garrett and saw that his intense gaze lingered a moment longer than necessary in the direction of the rocker. Slowly one corner of his mouth lifted in a lopsided grin.

Goodness, she thought, if only this moment could pass her by. Never, she promised herself fervently, would she ever be so neglectful again. "Tidy" would be her middle name. But instead of listening to her plea, the present seemed to linger into the longest seconds of her life as Garrett's hot, penetrating gaze once again swung to the wicker rocker and then back to her face. Her complexion flamed to life.

"I wasn't expecting to have company in my bedroom," she blurted out. Then her face became even hotter.

"Oh? What a pity," he replied, still grinning. "And here I was beginning to envy the lucky guy."

"There is no lucky guy," Whitney quickly replied, wondering how in the heck she had gotten into this conversation with him in the first place. At some point hadn't they been discussing his abilities as a father? Then how had they ended up talking about bras and bedrooms and someone else's luck? Damn! *She* certainly wasn't having any luck. At least, not in the past half hour or so.

"I have oatmeal," Whitney said as she turned for the door.

"Oatmeal?" Garrett repeated, watching as she strolled past him. "For what?"

"For Elsbeth's supper," she exclaimed. "What else?"

"Oh." Then he gave her that obnoxious grin again. The one that always made her heart go bonkers. "I thought maybe you wanted to smear the stuff on your face. Don't some women do that?"

The glare she gave him could have melted steel. He held up his one free hand in surrender. "Hey, I was just joking."

She forced a grin. "I'm laughing. See?"

"Good. I'm glad to see you have a sense of humor."

The glare came back. "Are you implying I usually don't?"

He coughed against his fist, but it sounded more like a suppressed chuckle. "And I think now would be a good time for you to make use of it."

The glare intensified.

What, Whitney wondered, was she going to do with this guy? Wasn't he a grizzly? Then why was he so determined to make her laugh at herself, especially when she was so determined to do just the opposite? With Jeff, her brother-in-law, everything she had said or done had been taken so seriously. There had never been any lighthearted moments between them. Come to think of it, now that she gave it any thought at all, she couldn't recall ever having heard Jeff give a hearty laugh at anything.

"Okay," Whitney said with a sheepish grin, "I'll admit I deserved that. I must have looked a sight when you came in."

"Oh, I don't know," Garrett said, walking over to her with Elsbeth in his arms. He whisked his thumb across her cheek as though he were removing a small speck. Then he gave her that lopsided grin yet again, and her heart went ker-plunk. "I thought you looked enchanting."

Whitney couldn't help herself. She laughed out loud as a honey-sweet warmth oozed through her. "Okay, you win," she said, smiling broadly. "Now, let's go into the kitchen so I can fix Elsbeth something to eat. Look at her. She's so hungry she's gnawing on her fist."

Garrett gazed at his daughter. "She does that all the time."

"She's hungry, I tell you."

"Well..." he said hesitantly, "you're probably right."

"I know I am," Whitney replied confidently.

She led the way into the kitchen. Garrett paused momentarily in the living room to glance out a window. "It's still pouring down out there," he said.

"Yeah—well, at least the lightning and thunder have stopped."

"Does this part of town have problems with flooding?"

"Nothing major. But the ditches often fill up," Whitney said, looking over at him as she placed a small bowl of milk in the microwave to heat for Elsbeth's oatmeal. She tilted her head to one side and gazed at him. "You're not from around here, are you?"

Garrett frowned. "Is it that noticeable?"

"No. Not particularly."

"Are you sure?"

"Yeah. But why would it matter if it did?"

"Uh . . . well . . . it really doesn't," he replied. "I just don't particularly like to be noticed in a crowd."

Garrett's all-American good looks would make him a target for second glances in any crowd. "But maybe you do just a bit."

Garrett flinched. Whitney didn't know it, but that was the last thing he wanted to hear her say. "Why do you say that?"

Her eyebrows lifted. "Why?" she repeated.

"Uh-huh."

"Well—" she hesitated "—for one thing, you're tall."

"So are a lot of other people."

"True," Whitney said, slowly nodding her head in agreement. "I think it's probably your stance—the way you hold your shoulders at a straight angle."

"A lot of people hold their shoulders at a straight angle, too."

"That's true," she replied sheepishly.

Garrett frowned. He wasn't sure just how he'd accomplished it, but it seemed he had backed her into a corner.

Whitney cleared her throat as she attempted to smooth back her bangs. "It's your voice . . . yes, I think it's probably the deep sound of your voice," she said, looking pleased that she had finally found an answer for him. "You speak with such authority." She smiled and then shifted her weight from one foot to the other.

He liked watching her fidget. It soothed his damaged ego. Lord knew, she had put him on the hot seat enough times where his care of Elsbeth was concerned. "But I seldom have reason to speak out in a crowd."

"Well then, I give up," Whitney exclaimed, throwing up her hands in frustration. "I don't know what it is about you. Maybe I was wrong. Maybe you *don't* stand out in a crowd at all."

He shrugged. "For a moment there I was kind of flattered that you were observing me so closely."

"I was not," she argued back. "What it is about you that's different is that you're not from around these parts."

"I moved here from San Francisco, but I'm originally from the Midwest. I don't have any kind of accent."

"That's the problem," she stated. "No accent. So what attracted you to south Louisiana?"

Garrett drew his eyebrows together. *Distance. Safety from his ex-in-laws.* "Work. I needed a change of scenery and heard that construction jobs were plentiful down here."

Whitney shook her head. She wasn't sure why, but she had a feeling he wasn't telling her the complete truth.

But why should she care?

"Someone sure steered you wrong. The economy here is as bad as anywhere."

"I'm finding that out. That's why it's so important that I be there tomorrow for my first day on the job. They don't seem to come along so easily these days."

Whitney leaned against the counter and considered what she knew about Garrett. Something about him just didn't add up. He was gruff yet pleasant. He looked antsy yet confident. He was, she figured, a man on the move. A man with some kind of past. And if there was one lesson that she'd learned from her experience with her brother-in-law, it was not to trust in the final outcome of a man in search of himself. Because when he found the answers he sought, there was definitely no guarantee that a woman would be part of his life.

At that realization, Whitney took an extra second in order to promise herself that when Garrett did leave Baton Rouge, she would make sure he didn't take her heart along with him.

The timer on the microwave beeped. Whitney turned and removed the bowl of milk from inside the oven and began mixing in the premeasured packet of oatmeal. Suddenly she stopped stirring, glanced over to where Garrett sat holding Elsbeth and said, "I'm sorry. I should have asked if you'd like something to eat, too. Let's see," she said, mentally contemplating the possibilities inside her refrigerator that she could offer him. "I have plenty of sliced turkey. I'd be more than glad to make you a sandwich."

"Oh, no," Garrett said. "I've already imposed on you enough as it is. Besides, I'm sure the storm will be over soon."

"Probably," Whitney replied. "But in the meantime, I certainly don't mind fixing you something to eat."

What in the world was she doing? Whitney asked herself. Damn this man and his innocent-looking child. They weren't her problem. Just who had given them permission to barge into her life like this and turn her insides upside down? She sure hadn't. And it damned sure wasn't fair of life to do this to her again. Resigned, she knew what she had to do. A part of her rebelled against what she was about to suggest, but a secret corner of her heart rejoiced. "You know, the storm could easily last all night. They often do. If that should happen, you might want to leave Elsbeth here with me for the night."

"Oh? And where do you suggest I go?"

"You can go home. I'll be happy to watch Elsbeth for you."

"Me? Go home? I hardly think so," he exclaimed. "I've never left Elsbeth overnight at anyone's house."

"Well, there's a first time for everything. Besides, you can surely make the sacrifice, but you really shouldn't take her outside. She's too frightened of the weather."

Garrett shook his head. "And suppose I don't want to go home alone? After all, I might be afraid of the boogeyman."

"Oh, *please*," Whitney replied, making it clear she didn't believe him for a second. "Surely you can come up with a better line than that."

"What do you mean?" Garrett asked, sounding wounded by her statement.

"I mean, who ever heard of a grizzly being afraid of the boogeyman? Now, come on," Whitney said, an amused look on her face.

"I could sleep on your sofa."

"I think not."

"Why not?"

"The neighbors, that's why not."

"The neighbors? Are they sleeping here, too?"

Pretending to be completely exasperated, Whitney placed her hands on her hips. "Of course not. But they'll wonder why you are and—"

Suddenly embarrassed at voicing the implications, Whitney couldn't find the necessary words to complete her sentence.

"But it's none of their business," Garrett pointed out promptly.

Whitney took a deep, calming breath. "Well, maybe in San Francisco it isn't. But here it sure is. This is a small subdivision, and the neighbors love to gossip. And thank you just the same, but I don't intend to give them a reason to think that the details of my life are so interesting that they should be made into public knowledge."

"A bit uptight about certain things, aren't you?" he replied with a twinkle in his eyes. Her heart jackknifed to the pit of her stomach.

Carefully Whitney placed the bowl of oatmeal on the table and seated herself. She clapped her hands together to get Elsbeth's attention and then gestured for the child to come to her. *Be damned if she'd let this man get to her.* Elsbeth moved in her direction, and Whitney took her from her father. "Do you mind?" she asked, indicating that she wanted to feed Elsbeth.

"Be my guest," Garrett said, stretching out his long, muscular legs in front of him and realizing how easy and how right it felt for him to turn over Elsbeth's care to this woman. Since leaving San Francisco, he knew he'd become an overprotective father—but with good reason. He'd had to be as certain as possible that all persons he entrusted Elsbeth's care to were good, honest folk who wouldn't sell out his child's welfare in exchange for money, if they were ever offered such a deal by his ex-in-laws. He'd also needed someone who, should the situation arise, be the sort of person that would allow him time to explain his reason for disappearing from San Francisco with Elsbeth before passing judgment on him. If worse came to worst, he needed time to tell them about the kind of emotional control that his little girl was being exposed to whenever she visited her maternal grandparents. Hell, all anyone really needed to do was get a good look at the shape Greta was in. Unfortunately, his ex-wife was a shining example of what could happen to a person who was totally influenced by them. Anyway, he had a feeling Whitney Arceneaux wouldn't be an easy sell for anyone. Not even for his rich, self-righteous ex-in-laws. Not even for himself.

He liked that about her.

Actually he found he liked a lot about her, period. And that bothered him somewhat. But then, could he have chosen her for Elsbeth's baby-sitter if he'd felt otherwise?

Still, he wished Whitney could have been more like Mrs. Ortego. The woman was reliable and trustworthy, yet nothing about her had ever thrown his libido into overdrive.

But from the very start, something about Whitney had made him feel altogether different. Her soft blue eyes held a look of hurt innocence that made him feel as though his gears were being stripped from forward to reverse, then back to forward again without anyone having the good sense to apply pressure to the clutch. And hell, all he'd wanted in the first place was for his motor to stay in neutral.

Wishful thinking.

So much for control.

"I know I asked you this last night, but you didn't answer me. Are you still baby-sitting your niece?" he asked, wondering why he always found himself thinking about this woman, especially about the full ripeness of her lips. In his opinion, they were just slightly larger in conjunction with her other features. Just slightly. Just enough to make him want to consume her mouth...

Great day in the morning, he thought to himself, but he wished he could keep his mind on the present. What was wrong with him? She was just an average-looking woman, for heaven's sake. If he could only stop thinking about her pouty mouth. Better yet, stop thinking about her altogether.

Hesitating, Whitney gathered up every ounce of willpower she had. "No, I don't baby-sit my niece anymore." God, but it hurt to acknowledge that out loud.

"I'm sorry," Garrett said truthfully. "I can tell that whatever happened was very painful for you."

"Yes, it is," Whitney admitted without looking up at him. She drew in a slow, deep breath and scooped up another spoonful of oatmeal for Elsbeth, who held open her mouth for the upcoming bite.

Garrett pulled in his long legs and leaned toward her. "Want to talk about it? It might make you feel better."

"No," Whitney said, shaking her head. "I'd rather not."

"Well, is there anything I can do to help?"

Whitney shook her head again. "No, I don't think so," she said. "But thanks just the same for asking."

Garrett reached across the table and cupped Whitney's chin, forcing her to look at him. "It's just that sometimes you look so sad. I wish there was something I could do to help."

"Thank you," Whitney said, lowering her eyes from his penetrating gaze. "But all I really need is time."

Garrett freed her chin. *Time?* Was that all she needed? It didn't sound like much. But he knew it was more than he could ever give her. Hell, for all he knew, he might be long gone before the next rising sun.

And Whitney Arceneaux deserved more than a one-night stand.

Besides, so did he. Because one night of making love with her simply wouldn't be enough for him. Of that much he felt certain.

Elsbeth chose that moment to pick up the spoon Whitney had just placed in the bowl of oatmeal and begin banging down on the hard white plastic. "Da-da! Go...go...go," she chanted. Bits of oatmeal flew through the air and clung to the soft, shiny bangs hanging down over her forehead. A small glob about the size of a pea clung to one of her long eyelashes. She blinked a couple of times but never stopped her chanting.

"Lissy, quit banging the spoon like that," Garrett said, issuing the order gently but firmly as he rose from his seat. "You're making a mess." He took the spoon from her and watched as her face immediately crumpled into tears. "Now, don't start crying, honey. I'm not angry with you," he said, using the washcloth Whitney handed him to wipe her hands and face.

Instead, Elsbeth began to wail.

"She's exhausted," Garrett said apologetically, taking her from Whitney's lap. "I think the worst of the storm is over with. I'd better get her home and into bed. It's past her bedtime."

Whitney widened her eyes. "I thought you said you always ate supper late."

"We do," he answered defensively. Why did she always make him feel as though she were questioning his ability as a father? "We eat late and go to bed early. Anything wrong with that?"

"Why no, Mr. Bear," Whitney replied. "None that I can think of." She stood suddenly and found herself almost toe-to-toe with him. Her eyes slowly lifted to his.

"Whitney, I hope to God you won't mind what I'm about to do," he said, his voice huskier than she'd ever heard it. But then again, the pulsating vibrations in her ears could have been the reason for that.

"Mind what?" she asked, wondering why she was trembling like a small puppy left outdoors on a cold winter's night.

"This," he replied, leaning forward. And then in the next moment his warm, full lips covered hers.

Timewise, the kiss lasted less than three seconds. But it left Whitney feeling as though her legs had just turned to Jell-O. Warm, liquid Jell-O.

Then he was strolling toward the door with Elsbeth tucked safely in the crook of one arm.

Hesitating for a moment, he faced her before walking out. "Oh—and thanks for the kiss," he said, giving her a sheepish grin.

Whitney's heart pounded against her chest.

So much, she thought, for all her good intentions of not getting involved with him.

Because she knew without a doubt that all those good intentions—with her agreement to baby-sit Elsbeth and now this kiss—were seriously in danger.

"I have to be at work by eight o'clock. I'll bring Elsbeth over around seven-thirty, if that's okay."

She nodded. "That's fine. I'll be waiting for her."

With a sinking heart and a curious sense of anticipation, she knew that she *would* be waiting—for both of them.

Chapter Six

The next morning came quickly.

Too quickly.

Emotionally Whitney wasn't ready for it.

So why then, her inner voice chimed in, if that were so true, had she risen at the crack of dawn, climbed up into her attic and pulled out the guard rails she had used on her extra bed while Allison had been in her care? Not to mention the other baby items—like the high chair—that she had to struggle with in order to bring down. And why, her inner voice continued, had she gone to so much trouble when she herself had made a point of telling Garrett Wilson that she would baby-sit his daughter for only a couple of days—three at the most?

Whitney didn't have any conscious answers, nor did she want to have to search inside herself in order to find them. Somehow she knew that if she did, she would find them buried deep inside her soul and that it would hurt far too much for her to pull them out.

She should have taken more time before making a decision that was going to be so heart wrenching, she told herself. True, she believed in neighbor helping neighbor, but as far as she was concerned, this baby-sitting job was way beyond the call of duty. He'd had no right to ask it of her.

But he had, and like the little fool she was, she had agreed to help him. So now her best plan of action was to place one foot in front of the other until the next few days were behind her. If she had to, Whitney assured herself, she could do what had to be done.

Having made that statement, the first thing she did was to put up the two guard rails on each side of the bed in her extra bedroom. Next she went out to her patio and, using a cleaning disinfectant, wiped off the high chair and foldaway playpen she'd also retrieved from the attic. After completing that task and walking back into her kitchen, she heard a knock at the front door.

Glancing at her wristwatch, she realized that it was already seven-forty and that she had been awake for nearly two hours. The knock, she knew, was probably Garrett's. She took a deep breath and hurried toward it. She opened the door, and he barreled through it with Elsbeth in one arm and a diaper bag in the other. He promptly dropped the diaper bag on the floor near the sofa and faced Whitney.

"Look, I've got to run. I made a list of things that Elsbeth likes to eat. Her food's in the diaper bag. Here," he said, handing Whitney a sheet of paper with a list on it. "Generally she naps a couple of times a day. You can reach me at this number." He pointed to the paper. "She doesn't have any allergies that I know of."

"I was about to ask you that," Whitney replied. "And her doctor?"

"I asked the guy interviewing me for the job, and he said the company doctor was Carl J. Adams."

Whitney frowned. "Doesn't Elsbeth have her own pediatrician?"

"No, not yet," he growled.

There was the grizzly again.

"Why not?"

"Because I haven't had time to find one." He threw up his hands in frustration. "Because she hasn't been sick, that's why not. Why are you always so hell-bent on giving me the third degree?"

At his outburst, Whitney's eyes widened in surprise. But she refused to back down on a matter so important to Elsbeth's welfare—not even if the child's bear-of-a-father sounded as if he was ready to bite off someone's head. She might have been city born, but she had been country bred, thanks in part to her maternal grandparents. She wasn't afraid of some wild animal. Not even if it was a big bad grizzly bear. She placed her hands on her hips. "Well, at least tell me that Elsbeth's had all the vaccinations required for a child her age."

"Of course she has." Garrett narrowed his green eyes. "Just what kind of a father do you think I am?"

"I have no idea what kind of a father you are," she retorted, frustrated. It didn't help any that he was right in asking her about the other matter. Just why *was* she always on his case? Garrett might be a bit rushed at times, but it was clear he was a very loving and very responsible parent. And it wasn't like her to hassle anyone.

Self-defense, her inner voice whispered. Jeff had easily bamboozled her into believing in his every word. She couldn't afford to have that happen to her again. Finding fault with a man like Garrett Wilson, who just so happened, on top of everything else, to have more than his fair share of sex appeal, was a good way for her to keep both feet planted on the ground. Right?

Right.

"Actually I don't know you at all," Whitney said coolly. And then in the next moment she couldn't help but silently admit that there were times when she would have liked to know him better. In fact, much, *much* better. For instance, now, when his straight-angled, lean-muscled shoulders stretched tight the washed-thin fabric of the white T-shirt he wore. Not to mention the casual way he wore the red-and-white cap on his head. In spite of his grumpy mood, it gave him that kissable, boy-next-door appeal that was very hard to resist.

But, thank God, she could.

And she really couldn't have cared less about the way his broad shoulders looked under his old white T-shirt, anyway, she assured herself.

Oh, but of course, her inner voice replied in agreement. And India's an island in the Mediterranean, right?

Still holding Elsbeth, Garrett ran his free hand through his hair in an irritated manner. "Look, I've got to get to work. Could we discuss my credentials as a father at some other time?"

Whitney shrugged. "Certainly."

"Thank you," he replied with a mock bow. Then his features suddenly became very serious. "Look, there's one thing I want you to promise me."

"What's that?" Whitney said, standing perfectly still as a result of the sudden sternness in his voice.

His green eyes seemed to penetrate their way into her very soul. As always when he looked at her in that way, a sizzling heat ricocheted throughout her body, starting at her throat, then dropping to her stomach only to bounce back to her heart, and last but not least, falling to her lower abdomen. Any lower and she would have been knocked to her knees. "Don't, under *any* circumstances, allow *any* strangers near Elsbeth," he said.

Whitney frowned. "Well, of course not."

"And if you see any suspicious-looking characters hanging around the neighborhood, you let me know."

"I'll call the police," Whitney said, vowing solemnly.

"No, that's not what I want you to do. You are to call me first," he said. His piercing gaze looked even deeper into hers and Whitney felt her insides turn to the consistency of melted butter. "Do you understand?" he asked, pointing to the center of his chest. "*You are to call me, first, before you do anything else.*"

Whitney creased her brow. Obviously the man was serious. Dead serious. Actually he looked as though the whole situation was a matter of life or death for him.

"Okay, I'll call you first," she promised, still somewhat mesmerized by the stormy intensity of his green gaze. His entire stance had somehow changed. He seemed almost threatening.

Almost like a caged animal.

Or like a man on the run.

Whitney's heart accelerated.

Oh, for heaven's sake, she was letting her imagination get the better of her—*again*. This wasn't some Hollywood movie set. Man on the run, indeed!

She unconsciously reached out for Elsbeth, and the child came to her willingly. "Garrett, what's wrong? Is there something you're not telling me?"

Garrett sucked in a sharp breath. God, he wished he knew her well enough to tell her everything about his past. He wished he could have told her that just last week he had gotten worried after realizing that a particular dark green car with an out-of-state license had driven slowly down their street a couple of times. He wished he could have told her that his stomach had felt as though it had been tarred and feathered until he had seen the vehicle pull into a driveway three houses down from him and realized that the vehicle's occupants were obviously expected by those living at that address. But he couldn't tell her that. He couldn't tell her anything. Not now, anyway. But maybe someday soon...

Now what kind of a ridiculous thought was that? he wondered. Even "someday soon" was out of the question for him and he knew it. And he'd be a fool to let himself think otherwise even for a second. "Look, I'm just very cautious about certain things where Elsbeth is concerned. With all the missing children in this country, I'd think you'd understand."

"Well, I—I do," Whitney stammered. "It's just that for a moment there you were so frightening."

Her softly spoken words slapped away the force that had held him in check thus far, and he immediately relaxed his stance. He wanted to touch her so badly, he ached with the need of it. Yet he stopped himself just short of reaching out for her. "I'm sorry, honey," Garrett replied. "The last thing I wanted to do was frighten you."

Whitney hugged Elsbeth to her. "Well, you most certainly did."

That was his undoing. "Oh, God," he groaned, his blood pounding in his ears. He reached for her. "Come here."

Unprepared for this sudden change in him, Whitney slipped smoothly into his arms. Elsbeth, now sandwiched between them, must have felt the charge flowing between the two adults because she just stared in awe from one to the other.

Garrett groaned deep in his throat. God, he needed this. He needed Whitney. She felt all soft and warm, yet smooth and firm where it counted. And though she was slightly taller than the average female, she still felt more fragile in his arms than any other woman he had ever held.

Her hair smelled like wildflowers. But what affected him the most was the bewildered look in her wide, lucid eyes. It told him that while she had suffered through her share of heartache in the past, she still held the unconscious hope that she had another purpose in life, another fulfillment that was just waiting for her.

The woman had no idea what that die-hard look of hope was doing to him. But he did. It was what was giving him this sudden surge of energy. It was what was making him want to toss all caution to the wind and kiss her as she needed to be kissed. The way he wanted to kiss her.

And as far as her purpose in life was concerned . . . well, it seemed as though it was quickly entwining itself with his own. Some people would have called that fate.

But at this particular moment in his life, Garrett had no choice but to call it *bad timing*.

"Look," he said, his hand trembling as he touched her hair. Even to himself, his voice sounded husky. A part of him would have wanted to court this woman if things in his life had been different; the other part of him wanted her, period. And unfortunately for him, at the moment the last part was the one doing all the talking.

He had to get back under control, he told himself. *Starting now.* He dropped his hands to his sides and stepped back. "Look, I've been thinking. I'm not so sure your keeping Elsbeth like this is such a good idea. Maybe I should take my chances that they won't fire me from the new job and just call in sick for a few days.''

Whitney took a step back, her gaze widening even more as she did so. "You can't do that."

Garrett's gut knotted up. *Damn her for doing that to him.* "Look, honey, you lead a normal, everyday life. I...well, I'm different. I lead a nomad's life. Easy come, easy go," he said, deliberately lying to her. But he had no alternative. He *had* to frighten her away from him. He already had his purpose in life. Elsbeth's welfare. And nothing else could come before that. Certainly not his own needs.

Suddenly he knew he had to get the heck out of there—and fast. Before he said or did something he would regret. Taking two steps back, he said, "Well, I guess it's too late to change things for today. But remember what I said about Elsbeth."

Whitney nodded.

"Promise?"

"Promise," she replied, sounding almost breathless.

It made him wonder if she was as shaken up as he was.

Then he turned and hurried out the door, because if he'd allowed himself a second longer in her sweet presence, he might not have gotten to work at all that day.

For quite a while after Garrett had left for work, Whitney carried Elsbeth in her arms as she walked throughout her house. She wanted to give the child a few extra minutes to become more familiar with new surroundings. Then Whitney placed her in the high chair and gave her a graham cracker while she rummaged through the diaper bag Garrett had left.

She refused to think about those earlier, sizzling moments, when she'd wanted nothing more than for Garrett to take her—right then and there—into his arms, without any thought about consequences. She was losing her mind.

Thank goodness nothing like she'd imagined before had actually taken place! Why, just thinking about the sensual images—of him and her *together*—that had popped in and out of her head was enough to make her face blaze with color. If she had actually lost control and given him an indication of the things she wanted...

She quickly shook herself free of those thoughts and then realized that her telephone was ringing. "Hello."

"It's me. I was beginning to wonder if you were home."

"Hi, Sam. What's up?"

"What's up with you, you mean. I saw that gorgeous hunk of a man leaving your house this morning." Samantha laughed. "Care to explain the reason for that to your very best friend in the whole wide world?" she asked, placing special emphasis on the pronunciation of her last words.

"My 'very best friend in the whole wide world' wouldn't assume she already knew the reason before asking me."

"Oh, Whitney, sometimes you're such a prude," Samantha said, making it clear by her tone of voice that her feelings hadn't suffered in the slightest because of Whitney's chastising answer. "Lighten up, would you? This is the last decade of the twentieth century, you know. At least, for most of us it is."

Whitney sighed. "Well, knowing your feelings on the subject, I feel certain you'll be thrilled when I tell you what I've done."

Samantha sucked in a deep breath. "Whitney, you didn't, did you?"

"My goodness," Whitney exclaimed. "Did I what?"

"Oh, come on, Whitney," Sam replied in an exasperated tone of voice. "Not even you can be that naive."

"Now wait a minute, Sam," Whitney said. "I'm totally lost in this conversation. Apparently we're not on the same wavelength at all."

"Okay. Then I'll get right to the point. Did our neighbor across the street from you spend the night at your place—with you—or not?" Samantha asked.

"What? I can't believe you would think such a thing! I just met the guy."

"So. Love takes but a second."

"For you, maybe."

"And for you, too. You just won't admit it."

"That was a ridiculous assumption on your part—being that you're my very best friend in the whole wide world and all."

"Oh, yeah? Well then, let me give you the scenario I witnessed less than an hour ago. It just so happened that I opened the drapes in my bedroom to allow the sunlight to shine through and—"

"Oh, but of course," Whitney said, cutting in. "It just so *happened* that at that moment you needed more sunlight, right?"

"That's right," Samantha said. "Now, do you want to hear the rest of my story, or what?"

Whitney sighed. "Let's hear it."

"Well, *anyway,* lo and behold if I didn't see a man leaving your home by way of the front door. And another lo and behold if that same man didn't just hurry across the street and jump into the navy blue Cherokee Jeep that's been parked out there ever since Garrett

Wilson moved in. Now what would you think if you saw something like that happening at your next-door neighbor's house? And remember, we're best friends, Whitney. We tell each other everything."

"If I'd witnessed such a thing I would think that maybe my *best friend* was doing the guy a favor by baby-sitting his little girl."

Samantha was silent for the longest time. "Is that what you're doing?"

"Uh-huh."

"You're baby-sitting?"

"Yes."

"Oh, Whit, that's wonderful," Samantha exclaimed. "What a breakthrough for you."

Whitney smiled at her friend's outburst. "I knew you'd be pleased."

"Pleased? I'm elated. I know it was a big step for you to make. Congratulations."

"Thanks."

"Hey, listen. I've got a great idea," Samantha continued. "Do you remember just last week when I told you that Jim and I had bought a new camera? Well, Jim's been taking a lot of snapshots with it, but I haven't. Anyway, I was thinking of going to the zoo this afternoon and taking a roll of 'candid' pictures. Would the two of you like to come along for the ride?"

"Sounds good to me. What time?"

"Ah . . . let's say around two-thirty?"

"Okay," Whitney replied. "By then Elsbeth should be up from her afternoon nap. But we will be home before five o'clock, won't we?"

"Oh, sure. Actually way before then. Jim and I are invited to dine tonight with Jim's boss and his new va-va-voom girlfriend from New Orleans. I want to have plenty of time to get ready. I even bought a new dress for the occasion."

Keeping a constant eye on Elsbeth, Whitney shook her head and laughed. "Sam, you buy a new dress for *every* occasion. In fact, you buy clothes for 'in case there's an occasion.'"

"Well, I never have anything to wear."

"Try checking in your closet next time. You'd probably be surprised at what you'd find in there—

"Look, I've got to go," Whitney said suddenly when she saw that Elsbeth was now rubbing her sticky, cookie-covered fingers through her bangs.

"Me, too," Samantha replied. "See you later this afternoon."

Whitney hung up and smiled at Elsbeth as she hurried to the sink to dampen a cloth with warm water. "Was that cookie good, honey?"

"Good," Elsbeth repeated for her, articulating as clearly as a three-year-old would have done. But Whitney wasn't surprised. She had already recognized the child's above-average intelligence.

After all, Elsbeth had probably inherited her intelligence from her father.

Now why, Whitney wondered, did she think that? And why did he always invade her thoughts? Why couldn't he leave her alone? She'd be willing to bet just about anything that *she* wasn't always on his mind.

She was bugging the hell out of him.

Garrett went about his new job with a vigorous energy that he wished he could have used to give himself a kick in the rear. Lord knew, he needed it. He'd tried everything else to rid Whitney from his thoughts. Nothing had worked. For instance, right this moment, while five stories up and balancing himself on a narrow scaffold, she was in his every thought. It was crazy. Just plain crazy.

"Aw, hell," he muttered under his breath. Sooner or later, if he could keep his mind on the safety aspects of the job long enough to live through this one day, he was bound to get over these ridiculous feelings for her. Damn it, he'd make sure of it.

"Hey, Wilson."

It took a moment for the alias he used to register with him. When it did, Garrett glanced toward the ground and saw his foreman motioning for him to come down. Immediately lowering himself, he removed his work gloves and walked up to the man. "Yeah?"

"The head honcho wants to see you." The foreman pointed to Garrett's left. "That small trailer over there is his office."

The one window that Garrett could see on the small camper-trailer was caked around the edges with dust, which looked an inch thick, from the construction site. Looking back at the foreman, he said, "Oh? Is there a problem?"

The man shrugged. "You got me. But I don't think so. I think he's looking over the application you filled out. So you're a college boy, huh?"

Garrett frowned. "Is that a problem?"

The man took several steps back. "Not with me it ain't."

Garrett couldn't tell from the man's somber face if that was a good sign or not. But in all reality, he figured that being summoned to the head supervisor's office on the first day of a new job was seldom done for a word of praise.

Hell, he knew he hadn't done anything wrong, but then again he hadn't done anything right, either. Good grief, he hadn't had time. He'd only been on this job for a measly three hours.

Damn, but he hated this. One town after another. One job after another. Always on the move. It wasn't his kind of life. He yearned for stability for his own well-being. But more important, he knew he somehow had to find it for Elsbeth's.

Garrett knocked on the trailer door.

"Come in," came a gravelly voice from inside.

Garrett followed the order and found a gray-haired, medium-built man in his early sixties sitting behind a desk with papers scattered across the top. "You wanted to see me?" Garrett asked.

His supervisor glanced up at him for the first time. "Yeah, Wilson. Come in and have a seat," the man said, motioning toward a rickety-looking straight-backed chair. "And close the door. The damned wind is really blowing today. Look at the dust in this place." He took a moment to light a cigarette.

Garrett tested the chair's stability and then decided it could hold his weight. He sat down and folded his arms over his chest.

"Wilson, I'm Lyle Broussard, and after skimming over your application, I wanted to talk to you for just a moment." The man paused, glancing down at a paper he held in front of him. Garrett assumed it was the application he had filled out when he'd come looking for work. Broussard rubbed his forehead. "Well, first off, I must say that I'm rather curious. You state on here that you're an architect."

Clearing his throat, Garrett nodded. "That's right," he said, straightening in the chair.

"You're telling me that you actually have a degree, right?"

"I do."

Broussard leaned back in his swivel chair, causing it to squeak loudly. "I see." Then for what seemed an eternity, he didn't say anything as he studied Garrett's application. "We don't get someone with your education coming in here very often."

"Look," Garrett said, realizing he was going to have to give this man some kind of explanation, "my reasons are personal. Let's just say that I needed to get away from my old life-style for a while."

The supervisor shook his head. "Yeah, well, I know how that can be. Look, kid, I've been watching you for the past couple of hours and I'm going to continue to watch you in the future. So I'm telling you right now, I don't want to be disappointed. I've been in the construction business for a long time and I know quality performance when I see it. I also know a lot of people in this town. I could probably help you out if you were to decide to make use of that degree of yours."

Garrett was completely stunned. He had figured on getting a good chewing-out—for whatever reason he hadn't been able to figure as of yet, but he certainly hadn't expected this turn of events.

Broussard stood. Garrett did, too. Then his supervisor offered him a handshake. "Could that be a possibility for you in the near future?" he asked.

Garrett took the man's hand as he opened his mouth to speak. But then he found himself hesitating when the clear, sweet image of Whitney's smiling face sprang into his thoughts, scattering his brain waves in every possible direction just as the wind outside was scattering dust particles.

"I'm not real sure about that at the moment, sir," he replied, taking himself by complete surprise. Now why hadn't he just told the man the truth? That it was quite possible he would be gone within a couple of weeks. He'd stayed in Phoenix for two months and that had been too long. According to what his brother had heard back in San Francisco, his ex-in-laws' hired detectives had almost found him there. It was a lesson well learned. He wasn't going to linger in any one place long enough to let that happen again.

Broussard smiled. "Good," he said, sitting back down in his chair. "Then we'll be talking about this again real soon."

"Thank you, sir," Garrett said. Then, clearing his throat, he continued, "I'd better get back to work." Taking a deep breath, he headed outside. His insides were tied in knots. Damn it, he hated having to lie. It went against every principle he had ever learned. Against every principle he planned on teaching Elsbeth.

The trouble was, he felt he had no other choice at the moment. The rumors his brother was hearing back in San Francisco still had him pegged as the bad guy who left town so his child's grandparents wouldn't be able to see her. No one knew, nor would they have believed, that those same grandparents had tried to kidnap his daughter from him. But *he* knew it and he would never forget it. The fact that he'd arrived in time to spoil their plan had been sheer luck on his part.

And until he could feel a hundred percent sure that Elsbeth would be safe in San Francisco, he wasn't going back. There was too much at stake.

Chapter Seven

The trip to the zoo was disappointing. Within fifteen minutes of Whitney, Elsbeth and Samantha's arrival, a sudden cloudburst had them and other zoogoers running in every possible direction, looking for the nearest cover. For everyone's sake, but particularly Elsbeth's, Whitney was glad it turned out to be only a heavy downpour without the usual accompaniment of lightning and thunder.

With Elsbeth in tow, Whitney and Samantha ended up hustling their way to a small pavilion along with nine other people. After crowding their way under the narrow roof, Samantha kept shaking her head and mumbling that she couldn't believe she was having such bad luck on her one and only day off this week. Whitney, on the other hand, simply couldn't believe that Elsbeth would choose this particular time to dirty her diaper in a real big way.

"Sam, we won't be able to stay under here for very long," Whitney said, her voice sounding grave.

"What do you mean?"

"Look, just take my word for it. We need to leave from here as soon as possible," Whitney murmured, this time saying it in an even lower voice. Without moving her head, she scanned the expressions of those near her, hoping no one was paying attention to what she was saying.

"Well, it's too late to do that," Samantha said loudly, but the sound of pouring rain on the low-hanging rooftop just above their heads drowned out most of the surprised edge in her voice. She did, however, look over at Whitney as if she thought her friend couldn't possibly have it all together. "You've lost it if you think I'm going to strike out from under here and get soaking wet in the process just because you think it's a little too crowded. At least we're not getting drenched."

"Sam, you don't understand. We have a bit of a problem on our hands."

Samantha opened her mouth to reply, but then stopped and took a small whiff of air. Then, attempting to act casual, she leaned closer to Whitney and whispered, "Do you smell something?"

"Uh-huh."

"And the scent isn't coming from those flowers over there, right?"

"Uh-uh."

Sam studied Whitney's steady gaze. "Elsbeth?" she asked, lifting her eyebrows.

"Uh-huh."

Samantha visibly paled. Then, as though someone had suddenly shoved a steel rod up her spine, she jerked herself to attention. *"Oh, no."*

"Oh, yes," Whitney replied, hugging the little girl even closer. Kissing Elsbeth on the forehead, she smiled and said, "But that's okay, honey. It's not your fault."

Elsbeth, possibly because of her fear of the rainstorm, but more than likely because of the gentleness she heard in Whitney's voice, placed her head on Whitney's shoulder and began sucking her thumb.

Pretending to need a breath of air, Samantha began fanning the warm, damp atmosphere around them. "My, but it's stuffy under here, isn't it?" She made a point of smiling at everyone.

Whitney felt like laughing out loud. Sometimes it was almost impossible for her to picture Samantha ever having her own child—heaven help the little one.

"Sam, you're only making it worse," Whitney whispered, noticing that the rain was finally beginning to slow down.

And thank goodness for that, she thought. Most of the people under the pavilion with them were beginning to give Samantha strange glances.

And then almost as quickly as the cloudburst had begun, it finished. Without hesitating, Whitney strolled steadily toward Samantha's car, one goal in mind—to change Elsbeth's dirty diaper. Samantha, on the other hand, mumbled something about needing a cold drink and flew off in another direction as if a whole army of bees were following her. Ten minutes later she returned to her parked car and found Whitney and Elsbeth patiently waiting for her. By this time the late-afternoon traffic had intensified and the dark clouds from the downpour that had given the ground a good soaking only minutes ago could now be seen hanging low over the southeastern sky.

After driving away, Samantha glanced at Whitney. "You amaze me, you know that? You're so good with kids. Nothing seems to faze you. The little darlings can spit up creamed spinach on your best white blouse, they can smell up their diapers in the middle of a crowd of strangers—you just take everything in stride. How do you do that? I would be so embarrassed. Oh, for goodness' sakes, I *was* so embarrassed. I guess I'll just have to send my kid to potty-training school when he or she is six months old."

Whitney smiled. "Just wait. You'll feel differently when they're your own. At least," Whitney added with a laugh, "for their sake, I hope you do. But as far as I'm concerned, I just love babies, period. They're so innocent. So uninhibited. So trusting. When I'm taking care of them, they give back to me so much more than I give to them."

Samantha frowned. "Yeah, in the form of green dribble."

Smiling, Whitney turned her attention to Elsbeth, who was in the back, strapped into Allison's safety seat. Whitney had retrieved it from her attic just before she and Elsbeth had left with Samantha for their trip to the zoo. In a tender tone, she said, "But Elsbeth is such a sweet baby. She would never spit up creamed spinach on my favorite blouse, now would you, sweetheart?" Still smiling, Whitney hesitated for a moment in a way that suggested she was expecting Elsbeth to answer her question. Then as she faced the front again, her smile suddenly disappeared. "Oh, Sam, I really need to be so very careful in the next few days."

"What do you mean?"

Once again Whitney glanced back at Elsbeth. "I mean I could really come to care for Elsbeth if I were to let myself." She sighed. "*Really* care a lot. I'm just so surprised at myself. I didn't think I had that much feeling left inside me."

Samantha reached across the seat and squeezed Whitney's hand. "Then why don't you let it happen? I sure wish something or someone would put back the sparkle in your eyes that losing Allison took away. Lord knows, it's time. Then I'd know for certain that you were happy again."

Whitney bowed her head. Resigning herself to the truth, she lifted it and stared straight ahead at the oncoming traffic. She watched as Samantha made a left turn onto their street. "I'm frightened, Sam. That's why I can't let myself go with Elsbeth. Because I don't want to be hurt again. Because, just as it was with Allison, I don't have any claim to her." She shook her head in despair. "The list goes on and on."

"And perhaps somewhere on that list is the fact that her father turns you on just a little and that scares you, too?"

Whitney waited a moment before answering. "Yes. I suppose it does."

"But just a little, though, right?"

Whitney nodded without actually looking in Samantha's direction. "Right."

Samantha smiled. "Yeah, right," she said, pulling into her driveway at a speed that would have alarmed any other passenger but Whitney—she'd become accustomed to Sam's driving long ago. Sam braked to a halt. "And everyone knows that my dream-come-true in life is to be more like Mother Goose."

Whitney climbed out of the car and was opening the back door to get Elsbeth when she looked up and saw Garrett sprinting across the street with an angry—de-

cidedly grizzly—look on his face. She was so surprised
to see him already home from work that she just stood
there, gaping as he approached.

"Where in the hell have you been?" he growled. "I've
been going crazy with worry."

"But why are you home so early?" she replied, over-
whelmed by his sudden appearance. "I didn't think
you'd be back until at least five-thirty."

"Yeah, well, it rained at the job site. We got off
early," he snapped, running a frustrated hand through
his hair. "But never mind about me. Where have you
been? Your car was here, so I had no idea you weren't
somewhere in the neighborhood. I've been up and down
the street looking for you. I was thinking about breaking a window in your house to get inside."

"I'm s-sorry," she stammered. "I—I didn't think—"

"You sure as hell didn't, lady. Who gave you permission to take off like that with my daughter without in-
forming me?"

"I—I—"

Oh God, he was right, Whitney thought. She should
have told him before leaving with Elsbeth. Especially
when the trip had involved a vehicle. The very least she
could have done was leave him a note. Why, if she'd
bothered to stop and think about it, she would have realized that she and Samantha could easily have been delayed on the return home. They could have had car
trouble. Or there could have been a traffic jam. Simply
put, she had overstepped her authority. It was just that
with Allison, no one had ever questioned any decision
she'd made concerning her niece's whereabouts.

But this child wasn't Allison. And she should have
known better than to take matters into her own hands.

See, she told herself. You're already starting to think of Elsbeth as your own, and you're headed for painful mistakes. Remember your place. You're just the babysitter, not the child's mother.

Whitney met her neighbor's steady, angry gaze. "You're right, Garrett. I should have asked your permission before taking Elsbeth to the zoo. I apologize. It won't happen again."

His eyes widened. "The zoo?"

"Yes. But she didn't get wet when it rained, if that's what you're thinking. We were able to find shelter quickly."

"I planned to take her to the zoo. How did you know that?"

"I—I didn't know," Whitney stammered. "It was Samantha's idea. But we didn't see very much of the animals before the downpour stopped us. Only the monkeys."

"Did she enjoy them?"

"Who?"

"Elsbeth—the monkeys."

"Oh—yes—she loved them."

"Then we'll have to go again," Garrett said.

"I think you should."

"Would Saturday afternoon be okay with you?"

Whitney blinked in surprise. "Saturday?"

Samantha, who had been standing some ten feet away, chose that moment to clear her throat. "Well, hurry up, Whitney. The man probably doesn't have all day to wait for your answer."

Garrett reached inside and released Elsbeth from her safety seat. "Look, it's no big deal if you have other plans," he said, lifting the little girl into his arms and hugging her momentarily.

"I don't, and Saturday afternoon would be just fine," Whitney replied, feeling so weak-kneed and off balance because of his nearness she considered leaning against the side of Sam's apple red car for support. Who would have thought that a guy dressed in a pair of dusty old blue jeans and a sweaty T-shirt could look so attractive after a long, hard day at physical labor? Yet all her senses were full of him—and still, she wanted more.

And more.

And more.

And Sam was right. That scared her senseless.

No man had ever made her feel like this before.

For that matter, no man had ever really bothered with her feelings, one way or the other. Not ever. Not her father. Not Jeff. And to believe that this man—this sometimes grizzly-bear-of-a-man—was different from the others would be foolish. It would simply be too big a chance for her to take with her already broken heart.

Whitney cleared her throat. "I have a few questions about Elsbeth's schedule written down on a tablet at my house that I'd like to talk to you about if you have time to come by for a moment."

"Yeah, sure," he said, studying her intensely. "I figured we'd have a few things to discuss. So how was your first day with her?"

"Elsbeth is such a good baby, and for the most part, everything went smoothly," Whitney answered warmly. "As soon as she became familiar with her surroundings, she began walking all through the house. She's at that age, though, where you have to watch her at all times, so I kept a special eye on her whenever I let her leave the play area I'd closed off for her."

"Yeah, she's a real handful. Especially ever since she started walking."

"How old was she when she took her first steps?" Whitney asked, using her hand to shield her eyes from the bright afternoon sun that had just rolled out from behind a small group of clouds. Undoubtedly the rainy conditions for today were quickly dissolving. So was Garrett's temper.

"Almost eleven months old," Garrett said with a smile, his gaze beaming with pride as he looked at Elsbeth. Using his fingers, he combed backed her long bangs. "She'd been pulling herself up for weeks, using the furniture and anything else she could find for support. Then one day she just let go of the sofa, took three quick steps and then fell sitting down. I couldn't believe it. But that was enough to give her the confidence she needed to try again."

"That's what I love about children. Their willingness to try again," Whitney replied. Unable to stop herself, she reached out and touched Elsbeth's arm.

Garrett tilted his head to one side and studied her. "What exactly are you saying, Whitney? Aren't *you* willing to get up and try again when you fail?"

"We weren't talking about me."

"Well, we are now."

"Not anymore, we're not," Whitney said, looking off in another direction. "So, have you heard from Mrs. Ortego?"

Garrett smirked. "You're using an old trick to avoid giving me an answer. It's called changing the subject."

"Actually it's called picking a topic of mutual interest."

"Oh," he said with a nod, "so that's what they're calling it these days."

Whitney cut her eyes back in his direction. "Well, have you heard from her?" she asked.

"No, not yet. Maybe she'll call tonight."

"I certainly hope so," Whitney replied, knowing full well that she was going to regret the day that Elsbeth's permanent baby-sitter returned to town and she wasn't needed any longer as a replacement. Even knowing that she would be busy with her bookkeeping each day after Elsbeth went home didn't change her mind. But she wasn't willing to share those kinds of feelings with anyone. Certainly not with Garrett. There were already too many times when he seemed to know her innermost thoughts.

Garrett was still studying her intently. "Look, did anything out of the ordinary happen today? Any strangers hanging around that drew your attention?"

"Only at the zoo," Whitney replied, gazing back at him with a *why-are-you-always-so-worried?* look on her face. To her way of thinking, he seemed to be overly concerned with Elsbeth's welfare. But then, Whitney reminded herself, she needed to take into consideration the fact that he was a single parent, trying to do his best. "And only because Elsbeth chose an awkward time to dirty her diaper. And even then, only because Samantha overreacted to it."

Garrett continued to gaze at her, only now he looked as though he was having difficulty understanding her. "What does Samantha have to do with anything?"

"Nothing. Absolutely nothing. That's my point. Nothing 'out of the ordinary' happened today. Now are you satisfied?"

Something smotheringly hot seemed to flare to life in the depths of his green eyes. "Not quite. But I guess for now it'll just have to do."

Somehow Whitney knew that his words pertained to much more than just their immediate conversation.

Somehow she knew that he was talking about himself—and her—and satisfaction guaranteed. And all she had to do was say yes.

All she had to do was crawl into his bed, warm and willing.

Like hell she would.

This wasn't some kind of game she was playing. Her future happiness—however slight it might be—was at stake here. Not to mention her battered pride.

So why then, she wondered frantically, if all her thoughts about him—about most men in general—were so true, did she still have this naked, primitive need gnawing at her like a starving animal?

Whitney noticed that Samantha had already disappeared inside her house. With trembling hands, she shoved the pink-and-blue strap of Elsbeth's diaper bag over one shoulder and turned for home. Carrying Elsbeth in his arms, Garrett followed.

"Are you upset with me about something?" he asked.

"Should I be?"

He caught up with her, and they walked along side by side for the rest of the way. "Well, I don't know exactly. I mean, I know I can be overbearing sometimes—possibly even a jerk—especially where Elsbeth is concerned. But look, my concern for my daughter has nothing to do with you or your ability to care for her. I think you do a great job. Otherwise, I can assure you, I wouldn't leave her in your care. You have my total trust," he added with one of those smiles that had a way of making the ground beneath Whitney's feet feel as though it were moving at two hundred miles per hour.

A grizzly one minute.

A teddy bear the next.

"Really?" she said, grinning back.

"Really."

Whitney's smile faltered. Once Jeff had said something very similar to her. Once she had believed that he meant it. Bracing herself inwardly, she asked, "Why doesn't Elsbeth's mother ever ask about her? Doesn't she ever try to see her?"

Garrett's grin evaporated. He looked straight ahead. Then, after a second he said, "Well, I'm not sure how to answer that. Last I heard her parents had sent her away to Europe."

"Sent her away? You make it sound like she's still a child."

"To her parents, she is. And in many ways they're right. But the real problem is they don't want her to grow up."

"Is that what ended your marriage?" Gosh, she couldn't believe how suddenly curious she was about his past.

"Partly."

By this time they had reached Whitney's house. She opened the door and gestured for Garrett to enter. "Would you like a glass of tea or a beer?"

"Iced tea sounds good to me," Garrett replied, seating himself at the kitchen table and then settling Elsbeth on his lap. Whitney got Elsbeth a drink of water and handed her a graham cracker. Then, reaching inside her refrigerator, she pulled out a pitcher of tea, added ice to a glass and placed it in front of Garrett. She tried to avoid any contact with him and thought she was successful, but just as she was turning away, he touched her arm, sending tiny tingles throughout her body. "Thanks."

"You're welcome," she replied hoarsely.

Then she watched him tilt his head back as he took the first swallow of his drink, all the while noting that her stomach seemed to bob up and down at the same rate of speed as his Adam's apple.

"Ahh..." he said, wiping the back of his hand across his mouth. "That sure hits the spot."

Whitney poured herself a glass of ice tea. "What's Elsbeth's mother like?"

Garrett halted his movements.

"I'm sorry, I shouldn't have asked that," Whitney said, feeling guilty for still wishing he'd tell her more about his past.

Concentrating, Garrett thumped his fingers alongside the glass he held. After a few moments he looked up. "Hell, why shouldn't I just tell it like it is?" Then, meeting her gaze, he said, "My ex-wife is an alcoholic, and our parting wasn't exactly on good terms. At least, not as far as her parents were concerned."

"Oh, Garrett, I'm so sorry," Whitney replied. Unfortunately she had firsthand knowledge of what alcoholism could do to a person. Not to mention the family members. "My...father was a drunk. He died six years ago."

Garrett took another swallow of tea. "Then you probably know what I'm talking about."

"Yes," Whitney said, glancing down at the floor. "I'm sorry to say I do."

The next several seconds were silent as both became locked into their own painful memories. Then Garrett shifted Elsbeth from one leg to the other. "The disease finally took its toll on our marriage soon after Elsbeth was born. Greta started drinking again, and within a couple of months, what little we had left between us was gone—destroyed. And now it's destroying her, too, but she won't admit it.''

"Did you try—"

"I tried everything. I even went to her parents, thinking they didn't know. What a giant-size mistake that turned out to be. They knew about her binges. They just chose to ignore them. Actually they made me into a bad guy for trying to help her. They said that all I wanted to do was to embarrass them in front of their friends by saying that Greta was a drunk. They offered me money to keep quiet.''

"My goodness," Whitney exclaimed. "What did you do?"

"I refused, of course."

Whitney wasn't at all surprised. Instinctively she knew that Garrett Wilson was a man of integrity.

Sipping on his glass of tea, Garrett gave Elsbeth another graham cracker from the box Whitney had left open on the table, but the child refused it. Instead, she rubbed her eyes as though she were sleepy. Garrett offered her another swallow of water, and she drank all that remained in the glass. Kneading his forehead, Garrett said, "After that, I tried again to convince Greta that she needed help, but she was already too controlled by her parents. They had her convinced that her behavior was normal. Excessive drinking, at least to some degree, is acceptable in most social circles. Certainly it was in theirs. So at her parents' insistence, she demanded a divorce. But by that time I knew it was over for me, too. I asked the court for custody of Elsbeth, and Greta didn't protest it. And by the time her parents realized what she'd done, I had sole guardianship of my daughter.''

"Poor woman. She needs help."

"And the scary part is that now my ex-in-laws would like to have my daughter so they can dominate her in the same destructive way. But I'm making sure that doesn't happen."

The determination in his voice alarmed Whitney. She sensed that something was terribly wrong. "Just what are you saying, Garrett?"

Suddenly his actions became much more formal than they had been only moments ago. He placed the empty glass on the table and stood, lifting Elsbeth from his lap and placing her in the crook of one arm. "Look, I've already overburdened you with my problems as it is. I'm sure you have your own troubles to deal with."

I most certainly do, Whitney thought to herself. And if the truth be known, you're fast becoming one of them.

Garrett hurried to where Whitney had placed Elsbeth's diaper bag. "I'll bring her back in the morning," he said using its hand straps to lift it from the floor. "And hopefully on time." Departing, he added over his shoulder, "Thanks again for the tea."

"Oh—wait," Whitney yelled out, springing into action as he reached her front entrance. All of a sudden she realized that she wasn't going to see Elsbeth again until tomorrow morning. "I'd like a moment to say good-night to Elsbeth, if you don't mind."

He turned back to face Whitney. "Ah—yeah, sure."

Whitney strolled up to them and clapped her hands together. "Come here, sweet Lissy, so I can kiss you good-night." The little girl practically thrust herself into Whitney's arms.

"Well, I'll be," Garrett exclaimed, shaking his head. "She's never become that attached to any of her other baby-sitters. Not even Mrs. Ortego." He grinned. "Of course, Mrs. Ortego doesn't have your freckles. And she isn't quite as cute as you are.''

Cute? He thought she was cute? Her complexion flamed to life at the thought. Hugging Elsbeth, she gave the little girl a big kiss on the cheek. "You look tired, honey," she said. "I guess the new routine and a trip to the zoo all in the same day was too much for you. I should have thought of that." Reluctantly she gave her back to Garrett. "See you tomorrow, sweetheart."

"And how about me?" he asked.

"Oh, I'll see you tomorrow, too." Whitney felt breathless—mindless—her emotions totally out of control. Surely he didn't mean what she thought he did!

His grin became mischievously wicked.

Oh, he did, for heaven's sake. He meant for her to kiss him, too.

He had to be out of his mind.

She lifted her face to his.

She had to be out of hers.

"Good night," she said on a whispered breath.

"G'night," he replied a second before their lips met.

And then Whitney's whole world exploded into a million bits of glorious color that slowly floated back down to earth, falling as gently, as lovingly as a lover's caress upon her hair, her face, her shoulders.

Suddenly she realized that it was indeed his long, steely fingers curving around her neck, pulling her close, demanding she yield to him. His tongue forced her lips apart and swiftly entered her mouth. Once inside, he stole something from her that she knew without a doubt would remain in his possession forever more.

Simply put, he stole her heart.

Garrett strolled into his house, knowing it was downright crazy of him to be feeling as though he were walking on air. No doubt, something—or someone—was going to depressurize him at any second, and he was going to fall back down to earth with a thud and right smack into the middle of the biggest mess of his life. Hell, his emotions were already in the biggest mess of his life.

Just one damned kiss and look at him. He was shaken to the core. Was he that love starved? Up until a few minutes ago, he sure wouldn't have thought so.

He settled Elsbeth in her playpen and then marched into the kitchen to get supper started. The Lord knew, if he were to put it off the way he felt like doing, his kill-kisser, super-sitter neighbor from across the street would probably be over here in no time flat, reminding him that Elsbeth needed a nutritious meal prepared for her each night and served on time. Damn her.

Damn himself.

How could he have let something like this happen? He knew the consequences. The added complications. The heartache that was sure to come. He knew all of it—and a whole lot more. But had he listened to his own good advice?

Hell, no.

Elsbeth started crying again, so he turned back to see about her. He checked her diaper and found that it was dry. However, when he lifted her from her playpen he noticed a few bumps on her stomach that resembled a weltlike blister. Mosquitoes, Garrett thought, hurrying to the bathroom to get a tube of antiseptic cream from the medicine cabinet. South Louisiana was full of them at this time of year. Probably at every time of year. And from what he could tell by their reddened condition, Elsbeth had only added to the itchy irritation by scratching at them. After washing his hands, he sat down with her on his lap and began rubbing a generous portion of cream into each sore.

"So that's why you're so restless," Garrett said soothingly. "Well, I would be, too, if some old mosquito had taken a few bites out of me. But this stuff should make the hurt all better, honey."

Elsbeth stopped crying but she continued to fret as Garrett wiped her face and hands with a warm washcloth.

"I think you need a nap, Lissy," he said, carrying her into her bedroom. After tucking her into bed with her panda bear beside her, he wound up the toy radio that played her favorite lullaby and then lightly patted her diapered bottom until she closed her eyes. Then he eased himself from the room, only to wait a few moments by the door to make certain that she was sleeping. Realizing she was, he went back into the kitchen to prepare supper.

He had this gut feeling that something wasn't right with Elsbeth, yet he couldn't quite figure out exactly what it was. Normally she wasn't a whiny child. Maybe it was just the first day of change in her daily routine that had her feeling so out of sorts. And then again, maybe it was just those darn mosquito bites that he'd seen on her abdomen. So often, when dealing with a kid that small, it was hard to determine what was really ailing them. Maybe she did just need a late-afternoon nap. After all, she *was* still a baby.

Garrett seasoned the chicken pieces he intended to bake and slipped them into the oven. He set the timer. Then he dumped a small bag of frozen green beans into a pot containing one cup of water and one teaspoon of chicken bouillon crystals. He sliced a ripe tomato into wedges, sprinkled salt and pepper on them and placed the dish inside the refrigerator until the chicken was done.

Lowering the heat under the pot of green beans, he went to take a shower. Usually, when he was exhausted, the feel of hot water pounding down on his tired muscles helped to revitalize him.

Tonight, it would help wash away the sweet scent of Whitney that still lingered in his nostrils.

Unfortunately it didn't work. Lately nothing worked. No matter what, some part of her sweet essence always remained on his mind.

He cut the water off, grabbed a white towel that he'd hung over the glass shower door and dried himself. Wrapping the towel around his waist, he stepped out, using his fingers to comb back his damp hair from his face. That was when he realized that Elsbeth was crying again.

He rushed into her room, flipping on the overhead light as he entered. "What's wrong, honey?" he asked. By this time he had reached her side, and the first thing he noticed was that she looked flushed. His hand automatically went to her forehead, then to her cheek. "You have a fever," he exclaimed, a hint of alarm sounding in his voice. Then he noticed that she had two more of those blisterlike mosquito bites on her face and three more on the inside of one arm.

"What the heck . . . ?" He lifted her shirt to examine her and found himself staring in horror. Her chest and abdomen were now liberally dotted with the horrible, blisterlike mosquito bites. Only now he wasn't so sure that a mosquito was the culprit. Apparently Elsbeth had a rash.

But from what, for heaven's sake?

Was this an allergic reaction to something?

And if so, did allergies cause you to have a fever, too?

He didn't have the answers to those questions.

God, but he wasn't prepared for something like this to happen to her, Garrett thought suddenly, an unexpected panic welling up in him. True, he had known that in all likelihood she would be sick from time to time. Small children usually were. Still...he wasn't quite ready...

He needed to take her temperature. He needed to call a doctor. He needed...he needed... Oh, God, he needed help.

He needed Whitney.

He picked up Elsbeth, rushed to the telephone and dialed Whitney's number, which he'd scribbled on a nearby pad for quick reference. His insides felt heavy, weighted down, while he waited for her to answer.

What if she wasn't home? Then what?

Fortunately he heard her pick up the receiver.

"Whitney!"

"Yes."

"It's me—Garrett," he said frantically. "Listen, you have to come over here right away. Elsbeth's got a fever and—and spots all over her body. She's crying and—"

"I'm coming right over," Whitney replied, immediately hanging up on him.

Garrett clapped down the receiver and hugged Elsbeth to him, trying desperately to console her. Walking to a window, he pulled the curtain aside and peeked out to see if Whitney was indeed on her way. He breathed a sigh of relief when he saw her rushing down the front porch of her house. He opened his door before she had a chance to reach it. The worrisome look on her face reflected his own.

"What's wrong?" she asked.

"I haven't the slightest idea," he said, worry thickening his voice.

At the sound of Whitney's voice, Elsbeth turned in her father's arms. Whitney gasped. "Oh, my goodness," she exclaimed. When she lifted Elsbeth's clothing to examine her more closely, a dead silence seemed to fall.

"Garrett, I think she has chicken pox."

Chapter Eight

"*Chicken pox?*" Garrett repeated as a shocked expression took hold of his features. He looked at Elsbeth, who returned his gaze with wide, saucerlike eyes.

"That's what it looks like to me. Has she been exposed to it that you know of?"

"No—yes—I mean, I guess so. I think Mrs. Ortego said something to me about it a week or so ago. But I didn't pay much attention. Elsbeth never catches anything."

"Until now."

"Yeah—until now," he repeated. "Are you sure?"

Whitney nodded. "And she's going to be miserable for a few days. Antihistamine would help relieve some of her symptoms."

Garrett frowned. "She has a fever, too."

Whitney reached out and felt Elsbeth's forehead. "How high?"

"I don't know. I didn't take it yet."

"I'll do it now."

Garrett turned toward Elsbeth's room and Whitney, after closing the door, immediately fell in step behind him, her concentration solely on Elsbeth.

"I guess that's the first thing I should have done," he said, stopping at the medicine cabinet in the bathroom to find the fever thermometer that he'd purchased a couple of weeks ago in case he needed it. He certainly hadn't expected to need it so soon. Then he started toward Elsbeth's room.

"Look, Garrett," Whitney said, following right behind him. "Don't be so hard on yourself. You reacted like any caring parent would have. You found your child ill and you panicked for a moment. That's a normal reaction. I would have done the same thing."

"Really? I find that hard to believe. Nothing seems to faze you."

Whitney wondered if her eyes were boring holes in the center of Garrett's back as they walked into Elsbeth's bedroom. "I think that's the second time today that someone has said that to me. I'm beginning to wonder if it's really a compliment."

Garrett placed Elsbeth in her bed as Whitney stepped up beside him to take the child's temperature. "It is," he said, point-blank.

Whitney really looked at him for the first time without having Elsbeth's immediate condition uppermost on her mind and she couldn't believe what she was seeing.

He was clothed in a towel!

Her insides started to tremble.

Good grief, she couldn't believe she hadn't noticed his state of dress before this moment. Had she been blind, or what? It wasn't as if something this outrageous happened to her everyday. In fact, this was a first.

What was he trying to do? Have *her* burning up with fever, too?

God, but he was lean and tanned and oozing with virility—and she was tempted to reach out to feel the dark brown hair that sparsely covered his chest.

To separate him from that towel.

But she didn't dare.

Instead, she cut her eyes back to Elsbeth. "Your father ought to get some clothes on."

Garrett looked down at himself. "Oh—yeah, maybe I should," he said shamelessly. "I guess I got sidetracked. Sorry." Then he quickly walked from the room.

By the time Whitney was ready to get a reading from the fever thermometer, he was back at her side, wearing a pair of old cutoffs. And no shirt. And she was trembling again.

The towel, she realized, had covered more of him.

But who cared? Or noticed?

Not her. Not *really*.

"Elsbeth's fever is a hundred and one degrees," Whitney said, her voice sounding different—definitely raspier—even to her own ears.

"Good God," Garrett replied, gripping the railing of the baby bed with both hands. "That's high, isn't it? We need to get her to the hospital."

"What we need is to stay calm," Whitney said, mentally telling herself that was exactly what she had to do. Elsbeth was hurting, and that alone was enough to make her hurt, too. But it was too late to worry about her own feelings. Deep down inside, she knew she cared for this sweet, motherless little girl—almost as if she were her own. Almost as much as Allison.

Maybe even more.

And just knowing that Elsbeth needed her right then more than she needed anyone else was enough to keep her calm and thinking straight. Call it motherly instinct. Call it "nothing fazed her." Call it whatever. She was in control because Elsbeth needed her to be.

"First we should give her something for her fever. If we have to, we can sponge her down with cool water. That alone usually lowers a person's temperature."

"Okay," Garrett said, now more than willing to turn over Elsbeth's care to someone he felt had his daughter's best interest at heart. Lord knew, he wasn't being much help. Whitney, however, seemed in total control. But if he were perfectly honest with himself, he had to admit that he didn't know much about childhood diseases. He could barely recall ever having suffered from them. His older brother, he thought, had gotten the mumps first and then had given them to him. "You seem to know what you're doing. What's our next move?"

Our? He made them sound like a unit, a family, working together as one, Whitney thought. "Where do you keep your medical supplies?"

"Everything's in the bathroom."

"Let's take a look," she replied, lifting Elsbeth from her bed so that the child wouldn't cry when they walked away. Ordinarily Elsbeth would have been perfectly content to wait for their return. But then today wasn't exactly turning out to be an ordinary day for the little girl. Actually not for any of them.

Garrett opened the medicine cabinet and stepped aside for Whitney to inspect. She found a bottle of chewable acetaminophen tablets for children, read the recommended dosage for someone Elsbeth's age and weight and then dumped that amount in the palm of her hand. "This should lower her fever and make her feel better."

She gave Elsbeth the medication, and the child took it without hesitation. Then once again Whitney felt Elsbeth's forehead. "I think I'll call my doctor and explain the situation to him."

"I'd appreciate it if you would do that. I don't have a family doctor for us yet."

"I know. I remember you saying that," she replied, handing Elsbeth over to him. "I'll go ahead and do it now."

Carrying his daughter, Garrett followed behind Whitney and stood close by as she placed the call. She ended up having to leave a message with the physician's answering service for him to call her back.

She hung up the receiver and turned to face Garrett. "About a month ago a friend of mine's little boy had chicken pox and she couldn't bring him to the day-care center for a whole week. So I volunteered to take care of him while she was at work. Anyway, her doctor told her to bathe him once or twice a day in tepid water containing a half cup of baking soda. And he recommended that she apply calamine lotion to the blisters."

Garrett made an expression of disgust. "Poor little thing."

"Hey, she's probably going to look worse before she looks better. So you'd just as soon get prepared for it." Whitney took a deep breath. "Oh, and by the way, did you have chicken pox as a kid?"

"What?"

"It's contagious, you know."

"Yeah, I know. But not for adults."

Whitney smiled. "Ask Samantha about the myth. She had chicken pox about three years ago. She got it from her two-year-old nephew."

That incredible look, similar to the one he'd worn earlier, now returned to Garrett's face. "You're kidding."

Whitney shook her head. "Uh-uh."

"But I thought . . . I've never heard of such a thing."

"It's rare. But it does happen," Whitney added. "I just thought you needed to be aware of that fact."

Dropping his hands to his side, he sighed. "Gee, thanks. What great news." Then he looked over at her. "Have you had it?"

"Yes," Whitney said. "Twice."

"What!"

She laughed. "Just kidding. Only once." Then suddenly she became serious and said, "I was eight years old and I'll never forget it for as long as I live. It was a horrible time for me."

"Why's that?"

She was silent for a few moments. "Because my father made fun of the way I looked."

"That was a cruel thing for him to do."

She shrugged. "Looking back now, I realize that he must have been drinking at the time."

Garrett drew his eyebrows together. "But that's not a good enough excuse. Where was your mother? Why didn't she do something about his behavior?"

"Because back then she was drinking almost as much as he was."

He gaped at her. "Both your parents were alcoholics?"

"Yes. But my mother sobered up when I was thirteen and my sister, Lisa, was fifteen. And the good part is that today she's still sober."

Garrett frowned. "Do you see her often?"

"Yes."

"And what's your relationship with her now?"

"We've become good friends."

Garrett shook his head thoughtfully, and it was then that Whitney realized why he was so interested in the outcome of her mother's life thus far. She walked up to him and placed her hand on his arm. "There's still hope for something good to happen between Elsbeth and her mother, if that's what you're wondering."

"That's hard for me to believe at the moment. Yet, for everyone's sake, but especially Elsbeth's, I hope you're right."

"Maybe your ex-wife will finally decide to get some help."

"You know, though, there are two sides to that story," Garrett said, sitting down in a rocker with Elsbeth. He took a deep, heavy breath and then released it. "And sometimes I hate myself for having the selfish thoughts that I do."

"How's that?"

"If Greta does get help, then there's always the chance she might want Elsbeth back."

Sitting on the edge of the chair opposite him, Whitney clasped her hands together in her lap. "Oh, Garrett, I hadn't thought of that."

"Yeah, well, I have. And I can't bear the thought of losing her after all we've been through together. We're a team."

"But more than likely you won't have to. The court gave you custody of her to start with. Why wouldn't they continue?"

He ran a frustrated hand through his dark brown hair. "Because that's just the tool my ex-in-laws are waiting for. If they can get Greta to take me back to court for custody of Elsbeth, then they will. Only this time they'll make sure they come out the winners. Believe me, I know what I'm saying. They'll do whatever's necessary to get Elsbeth—legally or illegally.''

"That's a pretty strong statement to make about someone, Garrett."

"I know," he replied. "But it's true. And I can't let that happen to Elsbeth. I'm totally convinced they would be emotionally destructive to her well-being. In fact, I'm willing to stake everything on it."

Alerted by his impassioned tone of voice, Whitney sat back in the chair. "Garrett, are you being totally truthful with me about Elsbeth?"

He stopped rocking, narrowed his eyes and then leveled them on her face. "What do you mean?"

"Do you really have custody of her?"

"Of course I do."

"Then why are you so secretive about your past?"

By this time Elsbeth had fallen asleep in his arms. Still he continued to rock her as though she weren't. "Because there's no point in getting you involved in something that isn't your concern."

"But I am involved. Can't you see that I care about Elsbeth?" Whitney asked, leaning forward. *That I care about you?*

"Look, this doesn't concern you. It's between my ex-in-laws and me. The less you know about my situation, the better it is for everyone concerned."

Hurt by his words, Whitney felt a weakening in her knees as she rose from her chair. "In other words, Mr. Garrett Wilson has his own, private way of handling things and he doesn't need your help, Whitney. Is that what you're telling me?"

"Yeah, I guess that's about it," he said.

"Then why did you call me over here?"

"Because . . . well . . . because I needed your help with Elsbeth. But that has nothing to do with me."

"Oh? So there's a difference between your needing me for Elsbeth's sake and your needing me for yourself?"

He stopped rocking and slowly rose with Elsbeth in his arms to stand face-to-face with her. "Lady, there's actually a big difference. And if you're not careful, I just might decide to show you what that difference is."

The promise of a teddy bear with the savage look of a grizzly. What a combination. What a promise. Too bad he didn't mean it.

And too bad she didn't have the nerve to challenge him to find out if he really did.

She averted her gaze. *Chicken.* "Well, then," she said briskly, "now that you obviously don't need my help with Elsbeth any longer, I'm going home. I have work to do." She moved toward the doorway.

With Elsbeth still in his arms, he quickly blocked her path. "You can't go yet," he exclaimed rather abruptly. "I mean—I still have some questions to ask you about Elsbeth's care."

Whitney stood very still with her arms hanging down at her sides. "Garrett, I left your number with my doctor. He should be calling soon. What more do you want from me?"

"Please," he said, his voice deep and his lean, sexy body still standing in her way. "Stay for a while. I didn't mean to be such a jerk. I apologize."

"You really are like an old grizzly sometimes," Whitney replied, her irritation with him new and stinging.

After a moment of silence, the corners of his mouth lifted into a slight grin. "Yeah, I guess you're right." Then he became more serious. "Look, I'll just have to keep saying that I'm sorry whenever I get that way. That's the best I can offer for right now.''

"Fine. I'll see you in the morning," Whitney replied.

"Please," Garrett said in a near whisper, "stay while I put Elsbeth to bed. Would you do that much for me?"

Refusing to think about how far she could go in her imagination with that one measly question from him, she simply nodded.

He walked out of the room and came back within a matter of seconds. Whitney was still standing in the same spot. He halted about three feet in front of her. For her own sanity she kept her gaze focused at the base of his throat. It took all of her control not to drop it down to the tantalizing waistband of his cutoffs.

"Look," he said, "you mentioned that Elsbeth will probably get worse before she gets better. And to put it quite frankly, I'm worried that might happen. She's never been sick before, other than a slight cold. I mean, I'm sure I can handle it . . . but I would feel better if you were here with us, just in case."

"Here?" Whitney exclaimed. "You mean as in stay here all night long with you?"

"With Elsbeth," he corrected. "With us."

"I can't do that."

"Why not? Elsbeth needs you."

"Elsbeth is resting right now. She just might sleep all night long."

His hands went to his hips in a determined way. "But she might not."

Whitney started past him. "Then call me if she doesn't."

She felt him grab her arm, and her insides quivered. Slowly she lifted her eyes and found herself gazing into his. "Please stay, Whitney," he said, his voice vibrating through her. "I need someone to talk with tonight."

She went hot all over. Apple butter had more consistency than her knees. "I don't think that would be wise."

He pulled her closer. "Why not? Are you afraid of me?"

"Should I be?"

His heated gaze poured over her face. "Yes, damn it. You had better be."

She shook all over. "Well, I'm not."

"But you're trembling," he said, his warm breath like a lover's caress upon her face.

"Because I am frightened. But not of you."

"Then of who?"

"Of myself."

His hand cupped the side of her face. Then his head began to descend toward hers. "That's really strange you should say that," he said, his voice a mere whisper. "'Cause I know exactly what you mean."

Then their lips met, and a second later their bodies were straining against one another. It was fast—intense—with a raw, unexpected hunger pouring forth from the both of them.

His tongue entwined itself with hers and did a wild, erotic dance that made her throb with desire. Whitney dug her fingers into the smooth, bare flesh of his back. He groaned and deepened the kiss. And then Whitney felt a sudden rush throughout her body that settled heavily—almost painfully—in her lower abdomen.

One of his hands was wrapped in her hair. The other was around her waist and held her crushed to him. His tongue was relentless in its pursuit of hers.

And yet she wanted more.

Never had she wanted so much more from a man.

And never had she been so willing to surrender what he was asking of her in return.

Even in the distance she could hear bells ringing and ringing and ringing.

Finally she managed to pull herself away. Or maybe he had pulled away. She wasn't sure. They were both breathless. But by now she'd come to realize that the bells she heard were, in reality, nothing more than the telephone.

"Garrett, it's probably the doctor returning my call." She moved away when he took a step toward her, intent on pulling her back into his arms.

Stopping, he reached to his left and lifted the receiver. "Hello," he said, sounding as though he'd had to run up three flights of stairs to get to it. He listened intently. "Yes, my neighbor, Whitney Arceneaux, called you on my behalf. I've just moved here recently, and my sixteen-month-old daughter has come down with chicken pox and I wanted to know what could be done for her."

Again, he listened. "Yes . . . uh-huh . . . I see. Yes, Whitney mentioned that giving her an antihistamine would help her symptoms." He covered the mouth of the receiver with his hand. "What pharmacy do you use?"

"Daigle's," Whitney replied. "In the River Oaks Shopping Center. And they deliver."

He repeated the information for the doctor. "And give her acetaminophen tablets for fever," he said out loud. "Yes, I understand. And bathe her in tepid water with baking soda mixed in. I'm to call you if I feel uneasy about her progress in the next five to seven days. Thank you, doctor." Then he began to give out the necessary information so that the physician could prescribe an antihistamine.

Whitney decided that this would be a good time to slip out without having to truly face Garrett after what had just transpired between them.

That kiss. That awful, most wonderfully disturbing kiss. She would never forget it. But, dear God, she prayed that he would.

How in the world was she going to face him day after day without remembering, in vivid detail, every splendid moment? Without actually feeling his mouth on hers, giving and taking what it wanted from her? What she so willingly gave?

She had already reached the door when she felt him right behind her.

"Just where do you think you're going?" he growled.

"Home."

"Why?"

Without glancing in his direction, she opened the door to leave. "I don't know if I can answer that question right now."

"You're angry with me because I kissed you, right?"

Whitney hesitated for a moment. "Partly."

"Well, you sure as heck kissed me back, lady. Or have you conveniently forgotten that little fact?"

"No, I haven't forgotten. That part has me upset with myself."

"Look, if I promise to back off, will that make you feel better about staying for a while? We won't even discuss how hot that kiss made the both of us."

Whitney's face flamed to life. Thank God she hadn't turned around to face him. Staring at the doorframe only inches away, she said, "Going home is what will make me feel better."

"I don't think so, Whitney. I think you're running scared."

She whirled around. "And what about you? Aren't you running, too, Garrett? As a matter of fact, don't answer that because I already know that you are. I just haven't been able to figure out from what."

He paled. "What do you mean? Has someone approached you about me?"

Whitney widened her eyes. "Why, no. Anyway, who would do such a thing?"

"No one. It was the way you said what you did."

"But you said—"

"Leave it alone, Whitney," he said abruptly. "For your own sake."

She narrowed her eyes. "Is that a threat?"

For a split second he clenched his teeth together. "No, damn it, it's not a threat." Then, suddenly grabbing her around the waist, he jerked her against him. "But this is."

Once again her lips were crushed beneath his, and just as before, she felt the same raw hunger gnawing at her. And while she refused to surrender to the growing need inside her, she couldn't find the strength to pull away from him, either.

After several long, passion-filled moments that made her dizzy with desire, he lifted his head and gazed into her eyes. "Whitney..." he said, his deep, rough-sounding voice a mere whisper compared to normal. "There's something you have to know." Then he placed his forehead against hers. "I wish my life were different, but it isn't. I can't ever promise you anything more than the moment at hand."

"I know," she whispered back. "Somehow I've always known that was the way it would be with you." She closed her eyes, fighting back sudden tears. "But it isn't enough, Garrett," she whispered. "I know what I need from a relationship and—"

He cut her off by placing his finger over her lips. He kissed one corner of her trembling mouth, then the other. "I know what you need. I just wish I was the man who could give it to you."

She heard herself whimper. And then he was kissing her again, and she found her mind, her heart, her very soul singing a bittersweet song of what could never be. Because if she had learned anything at all from her catastrophic relationship with her brother-in-law, it was that she would never be completely whole in a love affair with a man if it meant having to settle for whatever leftovers he wanted to toss her way. What was hers to give to a man, she intended to give freely. But damn it, she expected the same in return from him. And if he couldn't give her that much . . . then she needed to face the fact that he wasn't right for her. It might hurt like everything to admit it about Garrett. God knew, but she was already in love with him. But then the truth usually did hurt some. This time, though, it was a million times more painful than she ever would have dreamed. That was probably why many people—people like herself—so often chose to lie to themselves instead of facing reality. She had certainly been guilty of that. But no more.

Using every ounce of strength she had, both physically and emotionally, she pushed him away. Then, fighting to regain complete control, she took a deep breath and said, "I'm going home. And I think it's for the best if we forget about what's just happened between us."

Garrett smiled a secret smile. If his green eyes had had the power to become liquid fire, then she would have been roasted to the bone. "Yeah, you're probably right." Clearing his throat, he stepped back. "It wasn't much of a big deal, anyway."

That hurt.

She turned to go, but he caught her arm. "Since Elsbeth's sick, would you consider staying over here during the day with her instead of my having to bring her over to your house?"

Whitney hadn't even thought about tomorrow yet. "Are you thinking that she might be more comfortable resting in her own bed?"

"Yeah, you could say that I was thinking along those lines."

She thought about it for a moment. "Then of course I will."

"You know, even if Mrs. Ortego comes back by tomorrow, she still won't be able to care for Elsbeth. Not for as long as Elsbeth is contagious."

"I'll take care of Elsbeth until she's well," Whitney replied. Then she turned and practically ran home.

Garrett closed the door behind him, walked to the nearby green recliner and dropped his weight down into it.

Damn.

"Damn. Damn. Damn," he said aloud. He didn't need this kind of complication in his life. He certainly didn't have the time for it. Nor did he have the heart.

And it was Whitney's fault. Because just as sneakily and as swiftly as a thief in the night, she had reached inside him and stolen it.

And hell. Things were going to get even more complicated for the next few days.

But in all reality, was it really her fault that his feelings for her had come this far? Or was he the one guilty of trying to move her into his life, one small bit at a time?

The answer he got surprised him.

He heard Elsbeth waking up and rose from the recliner. "I'm coming, sweetheart," he said. And then he found himself wishing that Whitney had stayed. And not just for Elsbeth's sake, but for his own, as well.

But for her own good—and for his and Elsbeth's, too—it was best if he forgot all about the way she made him feel inside.

He made himself a promise that he would do just that.

Chapter Nine

The next morning Whitney was up and ready to go an hour ahead of schedule. She had spent most of the night dreaming about inaccurate fever thermometers and antihistamine tablets that caused little girls with big green eyes to grow hair behind their knees.

What, Whitney wondered, made everyone think that nothing seemed to faze her where children were concerned? Since she'd learned that Elsbeth had chicken pox, her stomach had been in a ball of knots. Not to mention all the really weird stuff her subconscious had conjured up during the night.

She was willing to bet that Garrett hadn't had much sleep, either. But then again, she reminded herself, she simply couldn't allow herself to become overly concerned with him. Only Elsbeth mattered. Right?

Right.

Still, she probably should have stayed with them as he'd wanted her to. Garrett didn't seem like the kind of man who would ask for help if he really didn't think he needed it. So why, she wondered, had it taken her so long to realize that?

And why didn't she just admit that she wanted to help him? And not only because of Elsbeth, but because of who he was, and the fact that she had come to love him.

There. You've admitted the truth, Whitney. You've let yourself fall in love with him. How foolish of you.

But did that mean she had to be a complete idiot because of her feelings? After all, she did have some pride. Loving him was one thing, but telling him…well…that was something she could never do. Because if she did, she'd be setting herself up for another big hurt.

Her telephone started to ring. Thinking it was probably Samantha or another one of her friends, she hurried to answer it.

"Whitney, it's Garrett. Listen, can you come over to my house a little earlier than you originally planned? Elsbeth was restless during the night, and I hate to have to leave her by herself while I take a shower before going to work. I might not hear if she starts to cry."

"Does she still have a fever?" Whitney asked, trying to gather up her wits. Hearing his deep voice had scattered them like ants.

"A slight one. And she's covered with blisters."

"Oh, poor little girl. I'll be there in less than ten minutes."

"Thanks."

She finished fixing her bed and then checked inside her purse to make certain everything she might need for the day was there. She gave her mother a quick telephone call before leaving. Otherwise, Whitney knew, by this afternoon her answering machine would be full of messages asking the same questions over and over:

"Where are you, Whitney? Why haven't you called me like you usually do on Tuesday mornings?" After making sure her back door was locked, she grabbed her keys and headed out. After all, what was the use in lingering around her house? Elsbeth needed her, and apparently, in his own way, Garrett needed her, too. And she needed them both. Therefore, she couldn't think of one solitary thing she had to do that was more important.

She knocked twice before Garrett came to the door, carrying Elsbeth in his arms. Seeing her caused Whitney to widen her eyes. The child's face and limbs were covered with blisters, and she looked flushed.

"Oh, sweetheart," Whitney said, immediately reaching out for Elsbeth. "I wish I could make those old pox just go away."

"She's miserable," Garrett said.

Whitney glanced at him and noticed that he didn't have to be smiling for the laugh lines at the corners of his eyes to look deeply grooved. His brown hair was hanging in his face, and for a second she was tempted to comb it back for him. "You look like you had a rough night, too."

Giving her a half smile, he rubbed his hand along the back of his neck. Then he rolled his shoulders forward a couple of times. "I've had better, that's for sure."

"Maybe a hot, soapy shower will help. Have you had breakfast?"

"I don't think I even had supper last night. Actually I can't remember."

Oh, God, Whitney thought with a sinking heart. She felt like such a jerk. He had asked her to stay, and what had she done? Run away like some scared little bird. "I should have been here to help you," she said.

His tired gaze leveled with hers. "You should have been here, period."

"I—I couldn't stay."

"I know. You explained all that to me last night, remember?"

With Elsbeth in her arms, she turned toward the kitchen. "I'll get breakfast for you."

"Whitney."

She whirled back around to face him. Just the way he said her name made her stomach fill up with butterflies.

"Is that the reason you think I called you to come over here early?"

She inhaled. "I thought you called because you needed my help."

He shook his head. "You're really something, you know that? You think you've got everything—all your emotions—neatly stored in place, don't you? But is that how you want your life to be? Like one neatly wrapped package?"

"Yes."

"I'd have thought you would have realized by now that you're asking for too much."

Whitney grimaced. "There was a time in my life when I asked for too little."

"We all make mistakes, Whitney. Don't let the past rule your life forever. There's a happy medium in there somewhere."

And I wish it could have been you. "You don't have any room to talk. Your past haunts you, too."

"Maybe."

"Then what makes you feel qualified to give me advice?"

"My problems are different from yours."

"Only in your own mind."

After a moment he said, "Maybe you're right."

The heated, searching look he gave her caused her heart to jump into her throat. Anxious over the possibility that he might read her thoughts, as well as her feelings, she glanced pointedly at her wristwatch. "You'd better hurry or you'll end up being late for work."

For the longest time he gazed at her through narrow, intense eyes. Finally, appearing to have made some sort of decision, he quickly turned and walked from the room. Whitney took a deep, calming breath, went into the kitchen and, after seating Elsbeth in her high chair, fixed oatmeal for the child. Then she looked in the refrigerator and found cheese and eggs and decided to make Garrett an omelet. After toasting two slices of bread, she walked into the living room and announced just loud enough so that he could hear that breakfast was ready.

A couple of minutes later, he appeared at the kitchen table wearing jeans and work boots and a forest green T-shirt that looked like a second skin covering his lean, muscled chest. His hair was still damp from the shower. Her pulse leapt into high gear at the sight of him, but she willed herself to remain calm as she poured him a cup of steaming coffee. Then she did the same for herself and sat across from him. She gave Elsbeth another bite of oatmeal.

"When was the last time Elsbeth had her medication?"

As though it might help him remember the answer, he looked up for a moment at the round-faced clock on the wall. "Her next dose of antihistamine will be due at eight o'clock."

Whitney glanced down at her own watch and nodded. "I think the first thing I'll do as soon as you leave this morning is to give her one of those baths the doctor recommended. She might rest better after that."

Garrett took a sip of coffee. "I gave her one last night. The bottle of calamine lotion is in the bathroom." He picked up his remaining slice of toast and slapped a knifeful of margarine on it. "Whitney—I want to say thanks for coming over here like this. I guess I sometimes get so fired up and involved with my own problems, I probably seem insensitive to you. But I'm not really the grizzly you seem to think I am." He folded his bread in half and took a bear-size bite. He chewed several times and swallowed. "Really I'm not." He ate the last of the omelet on his plate.

Whitney had to grin. "Just who are you trying to convince of that, me or yourself?"

Finishing his meal, he stood, leaned over and placed a quick kiss on her mouth that took her by complete surprise. "Both of us, I guess."

Then he was strolling toward the door, taking her heart and her soul right along with him. "By the way," he said over his shoulder, "the omelet was good." He stepped onto the porch before turning to face her and Elsbeth. "I'll phone sometime later this morning to see how Lissy's doing. But in the meantime, don't hesitate to call at my job if you need me for something. The number's by the telephone."

I do need you for something. I need you to make love to me—right now. Whitney rose and hurriedly collected the dirty dishes from the table. "Don't worry about Elsbeth. I'll take good care of her."

He paused momentarily as though he had something he needed to say. Finally he said, "I know you will." Then he shut the door.

Sighing, Whitney sat back down in the chair next to Elsbeth and tried to get the child to eat the remainder of her breakfast, but she refused. So Whitney carried her into the bathroom, drew enough lukewarm water for a bath and added soda to it. For the next ten minutes she sponged the tepid water over Elsbeth's shoulders so that the treated solution could slide down her small body. Whitney knew her careful, continuous bathing felt good to Elsbeth because the child never complained the whole time. Only when Whitney removed her from the tub and patted her dry did she start to whine. But Whitney quickly applied calamine lotion to her blisters and then dressed her in a clean cotton gown.

"I hope you can sleep now, honey," Whitney said, sitting in a chair near the patio entrance. She allowed Elsbeth to get comfortable in her arms and then she began to hum a lullaby. Elsbeth laid her head against Whitney's chest, stuck her thumb into her mouth and closed her eyes. Within a matter of minutes, she was sound asleep. Whitney smiled in satisfaction.

But Elsbeth's peaceful rest didn't last as long as Whitney had hoped. An hour later she was awake and crying. Whitney rocked her back to sleep only to have her awaken again a short time later.

Garrett called during the morning and once more during the afternoon, at which times Whitney told him that Elsbeth was cranky but otherwise doing as well as expected.

However, by five o'clock both Elsbeth and Whitney were tiring. Most of Whitney's day had been spent trying to prevent Elsbeth from scratching the blisters covering her body. As a result of her continuous interference, Elsbeth had become extremely irritable.

Whitney had just finished giving the child another warm, soda-laden bath and had laid her down for a nap when Garrett arrived home from work. His eyes narrowed in concern when he walked into Elsbeth's room and Whitney turned around to face him.

"My God, are you all right? You look exhausted."

"Shh…" she whispered, practically tiptoeing to where he stood. She motioned for him to follow her. "She's finally asleep."

Garrett frowned but didn't say another word.

Whitney walked into the kitchen, slumped down into one of the chairs at the kitchen table and took a deep breath. "Well, she's probably gotten through the worst of it. Tomorrow should be a lot better. For one thing, she hasn't had any fever since noon."

"That's a good sign, isn't it?"

"I think so," Whitney replied with a smile. Then, choosing that particular moment, her stomach growled and her smile immediately turned to a look of embarrassment. "I must be hungrier than I thought," she exclaimed as a blush tinged her cheeks. "I guess I forgot to eat lunch."

"You didn't eat lunch?" Garrett repeated, walking toward the refrigerator. He opened the door and then immediately shut it. "Hey, I've got an idea," he said, now scanning through the pantry, which was located next to the refrigerator. He studied the different contents. Then, a pleased-with-himself expression on his face, he turned to face Whitney. "First let me get cleaned up, then I'll fix us both something to eat."

"Oh, no," Whitney said, rising from the chair. Her shoulder and back muscles felt sore and tight, a direct result of a tension-filled day. What she really needed was a good soak in a hot tub of water. *With Garrett soaking right alongside of her.* "You don't have to do that."

"Well, I have to fix myself something for supper. So why not do it for the both of us? In the meantime, you can rest," he said, reaching behind him for the refrigerator door without actually looking in that direction. "I feel it's the least I can offer you after the care you've given to Elsbeth." Then he turned and glanced inside. A second later he pulled out a bottle of wine. "No doubt we both could use a glass of this stuff."

"A gallon," Whitney said jokingly.

He chuckled. "You know, it's been a while since I've had anyone over for dinner." Placing the wine bottle on the counter and tucking the tips of his fingers in the back pockets of his jeans, he stood facing her for a moment and grinned. "And I want to let you know right off that I'm not the world's greatest chef. But as one of the guys I work with would say, I can toss a good salad when I have to."

Whitney laughed. "Sounds good to me."

He opened the bottle of wine and poured them each a glass. "Here," he said, handing her a goblet. "Sip on this while I take a shower."

Whitney took her first swallow, and the cool liquid had a warming effect as it slid down her throat. Actually she already felt warm from head to toe. This teddy-bear side of Garrett really was having a strong effect on her.

It's called the hots, Whitney, her inner voice chimed in. And boy, do you ever have 'em.

Whitney's stomach sank to her knees. Incredibly she knew that there was no use in arguing the point. She just couldn't believe that she had fallen for him so easily and so hard after all the warnings she'd given herself.

Garrett poured himself more wine and offered to do the same for her. As he did so, he gripped her wrist and held her hand steady. Whitney began to wonder if her body was going to liquify right there at his feet.

He released her hand and returned the remainder of the wine to the refrigerator. "I'm going to take a shower now," Garrett said, his voice sounding deep and gruff. He moved swiftly from her, as though he was suddenly in a hurry to leave the room. Pointing through the doorway to the green, man-size recliner placed in one corner of the living room, he added, "And you rest." Then he slipped from her sight.

Whitney sank into the chair and used the weight of her body to force it into a reclining position. She took a swallow of wine and then placed the glass on the table next to the recliner. After a few moments she dozed off, only to find herself springing back to attention when she heard a small child crying.

Whitney hurried to Elsbeth's bedside and found her in a restless sleep. So, just as she had done earlier that afternoon, Whitney picked up the child, carried her into Garrett's room and placed her in the center of the full-size bed. Then she lay next to Elsbeth and cradled the child in her arms. Whitney had discovered that if she lay next to Elsbeth, the little girl seemed to rest better and for a longer period of time. Whitney was hoping it worked again this time.

And it did.

Within a matter of minutes, both of them were sound asleep.

Garrett emerged from the bedroom dressed in a pair of jogging shorts. He couldn't help but wonder if he was losing his mind by asking Whitney to stay over for supper. After all, it wasn't as though he owed her more than he did any of the other sitters he'd had in the past. Why keep her here when it was obvious to anyone who cared to pay any attention at all that her presence knocked his equilibrium off balance?

Actually she knocked everything about him off balance. His way of thinking. His way of feeling. He felt like a total mess when she was around. Like a kid on prom night who realizes too late that he's forgotten to buy his date a corsage to match the colors in her dress.

A big mistake.

That's what he was making. So why didn't he stop himself? Why did he continue when he knew he had no future with her? After all, he reminded himself, she deserved so much more than he could ever give her.

With the damp towel that he'd used to dry himself after showering now hanging around his neck, Garrett walked right through his bedroom without glancing toward the bed that was placed against an opposite wall.

He expected to find Whitney in the living room and was somewhat surprised when he got there and saw that the recliner he'd indicated for her to rest in was empty. He strolled into the kitchen and found it empty, too.

Where had she gone? he wondered, a smothering feeling suddenly sliding down his throat.

"Whitney?" he called out. She didn't respond. "Whitney?" he repeated in a louder tone, glancing out the window over the kitchen sink. He didn't see her in the yard, either.

She'd left and gone home, damn it. Again.

"Aw, the hell with it," he said out loud. It was for the best, anyway.

His telephone started ringing. He answered it gruffly.

"Garrett, it's me," said a male voice that hinted at a slight West Coast accent. When Garrett didn't give an immediate response, the voice continued, "Garrett, it's David. Remember me, I'm your brother? Hello? Is there anyone on the line?"

"Yeah," Garrett replied. "You just startled me, that's all."

"Is Elsbeth okay?" David asked.

"She's got chicken pox."

"Sounds to me like you've already got your hands full."

"And that sounds to me like you have something to tell me that I'm not going to enjoy hearing."

"Damn it, Garrett. I can't tell you how sorry I am that you've had to go through all this for Elsbeth's sake. I wish there was something more I could do to help the situation besides relaying messages between you and your attorney."

Garrett's stomach knotted up. He and David had always been close, and he knew his brother better than anyone else did. And what he was hearing in David's tone alarmed him. Something was wrong. Something was terribly wrong. What were his ex-in-laws up to now?

"What is it?"

"Well, we're not absolutely sure yet. You know how underhanded the people you're dealing with can be."

"Yes, yes, I know. Get on with it, David."

"Well, rumor has it that Greta's checked herself into an exclusive treatment center someplace in Europe without getting permission from her old man. But no one seems to know for sure if it's the truth. Anyway, it's been passed on to me that there is a great deal of activity going on at the Ramsey estate. Lots of big cars coming and going. One particular vehicle was identified as the one belonging to a judge who's had dealings with them in the past."

"Probably Judge Hawkens," Garrett replied. "He and Greta's father go back a long way. Fraternity brothers, something like that."

"Well, I have to tell you, Garrett," David continued heavily, "it's got everyone here who cares about you and Elsbeth worried sick. We all know what the Ramseys are capable of doing."

Yeah, Garrett thought, the feeling of disappointment inside him now turning into total distress.

But damn it, hadn't he made it this far? Wasn't Elsbeth well loved? And well fed? And wasn't Whitney taking excellent care of her during the times that he couldn't?

Whitney. Dear God, how had he allowed her to touch him so deeply that even at a time like this he would think of her?

The knot in Garrett's stomach turned into a viselike grip. "Keep on it, David, and let me know the minute you find out anything more."

"I will. Oh, and Garrett, how's the money situation? Do you need for me to send you any?"

"No. I'm too afraid that it could end up being traced. Besides, I've been able to continue working in spite of Elsbeth's illness. My neighbor across the street is taking care of her."

"Can that person be trusted?"

"Implicitly."

"You sure?"

"Positive."

David sighed. "Okay. I'll be in touch."

After hanging up the telephone, Garrett remained standing there for the longest time. For the first time in months he found himself having to admit that he couldn't continue this life-style much longer. It was getting the best of him, and before long it would do the same to Elsbeth, too. He couldn't let that happen. But at the same time, he couldn't let his ex-in-laws take Elsbeth away. He just couldn't.

There had to be an answer, Garrett thought. Sooner or later something had to give. And from the uneasy feeling in the pit of his stomach, he felt quite certain it was going to be a lot sooner than he had originally expected.

And Whitney. What was he going to do about her?

He was going to have to leave her, that's what. God, he didn't want to have to do that. But what choice did he have? It would be selfish of him to willingly get her involved with his problems. It was obvious that she was recovering from her own painful past; she didn't need the mess in his life adding any extra complications to hers. Besides, he already had enough to feel guilty about as it was.

Towel-drying his hair, he headed for Elsbeth's bedroom to check on her. Frowning in confusion when he found her bed empty, he stood there, gazing around. Even her panda bear was gone.

Suddenly it was as though a volcano of realization erupted inside him. My God, both Elsbeth and Whitney were missing. Could it mean . . . ?

No, his inner voice hurriedly piped in. Whitney would not have taken Elsbeth. They were here—together—somewhere. All he had to do was look for them.

And he began his search to do just that, first by glancing in the bathroom just to make sure they weren't there.

The tightening in the pit of his stomach continued. Dear God, he prayed, please don't let me be wrong about Whitney.

He tossed the towel from around his neck and into the tub, then quickly crossed the hall into his bedroom.

And there he found the two lost treasures in his life, nestled together and sound asleep on his bed. His heart squeezed tight with love. To be able to lie down beside them and cradle them in his arms forever would have been his greatest desire.

He walked to the side of the bed, leaned over and gently pushed the hair back from Elsbeth's face. Then he did the same to Whitney. With a bitter pang, he acknowledged that he couldn't keep them here like this. At least, not forever—time moved on and nothing stayed the same, no matter what. But for a while, while they slept and he kept watch, he would hold them tenderly, protectively, with his eyes, with his very soul. And no matter what happened in the future, no one was going to be able to take these few special moments away from him. They would be his for all eternity.

He eased himself onto the mattress, right alongside Elsbeth. Lying down, he propped his head up with one hand and gently placed his other arm across Elsbeth and Whitney. His goal wasn't to awaken them, and he smiled in satisfaction when neither female gave any indication that she felt his presence. Then he allowed himself the luxury of studying their every feature. And so intent was he at remembering every fine detail that he never noticed when his own head lowered to the bed and he, too, fell asleep.

Whitney awoke with a start. She blinked twice and still she couldn't make any sense of things. She felt cool, the way she often did when falling asleep on the sofa watching television. But she had enough sense about her to realize that she wasn't on her sofa and she hadn't been watching television.

She was lying on a bed in a strange, dark room, and the background noise she was hearing sounded like the humming of an air-conditioning unit...and someone else was lying near her.

And then finally she remembered where she was. Late this afternoon she had lain in the middle of Garrett's bed with Elsbeth. Only now it was dark outside.

She felt for Elsbeth and found her still sleeping next to her. No fever, Whitney thought, noting the coolness of her skin. Great. Then she suddenly realized that someone's hand, which up until that moment she hadn't been aware was at her waist, had begun to move up and down her lower back. She was definitely not alone with Elsbeth anymore.

"Are you awake?" Garrett whispered after a few moments, his voice thicker sounding than the feel of darkness around them.

"Uh-huh," she replied, too relaxed to say any more. "That feels good. Don't stop."

"I hadn't planned on stopping—that is, unless you wanted me to."

"No."

"Then I won't."

"Garrett—"

"Whitney—"

"You go first," he said.

"No, you go first," Whitney replied.

The bedding beneath him rustled as he eased up on one elbow. His other hand moved from her waistline to cup the side of her face. "I wish to God I could confide in you, Whitney. But I'm afraid you'd end up hurt in the process.''

"I think you should let me be the judge of that.''

His hand moved slowly downward until it came to rest on her breast. He began rubbing his palm over her nipple in a slow, circular motion that seemed to gun hot oil into her veins. She groaned.

"I think, sweet Whitney, that you're already beyond the line of good judgment.''

"And so are you,'' she said, lifting her face to his. And then he was kissing her, and she was responding to him with a passion she hadn't known she possessed until that moment.

Chapter Ten

Somehow, without Whitney's lips parting from his, Garrett had managed to lift himself over her and was now pulling them both from the mattress. Together they slid down to the carpet, with Whitney ending up on his lap, straddling him.

"Oh, baby," he said hoarsely, "I feel like I'm going to explode if I don't have you."

His mouth was hot and seeking, his teeth strong and tantalizing, as he nipped and tasted her earlobes, her neck, her cheeks, her lips. His fingers began to unfasten the buttons of her shirt. She wanted him equally as much and let him know by answering his every kiss with burning, wild ones of her own. Their hands were on each other, grasping and pulling. Their breathing came in hard, fast pants and could easily be heard throughout the room.

Then Elsbeth began to cry, and their moment of unbridled passion was immediately harnessed.

Abruptly brought back to their senses, they needed several seconds to actually make the jump to reality, so absorbed had they been by the overwhelming rush of their feelings just moments before. With trembling, erratic movements, Whitney quickly fastened those buttons on her shirt that Garrett had managed to release. Still flushed with desire, she was completely mortified by her display.

How could she have acted so irrationally?

So shamelessly?

There. At least she'd had the guts to admit her actions for what they were. Somehow, though, that didn't make her feel a whole lot better about herself. If only she could look him in the eyes . . .

And then she found it an easy thing to do because in the next instant he lifted her chin so that she had no choice but to look at him. He kissed her softly on the lips. "Another time, lady," he said.

Then he gently shifted her weight to the carpet, rose and lifted Elsbeth into his arms. "What's the matter with Daddy's little girl?" he said in the concerned tone of voice that Whitney had come to expect when he spoke to his daughter. He was a good father, she thought warmly.

And he'd be a good lover, too. The throbbing ache that still raged through her body from his ardent kisses was proof of that.

Rising, Whitney pushed her hair from her face. "Does she have any fever?" she asked, now trying to tuck her shirt back into her waistband.

"I don't think so," he replied, his gaze meeting hers. "What do you think?" Then he gave her a half smile. Still somewhat self-conscious, Whitney returned it.

She felt Elsbeth's forehead. "No, I don't think she does."

Then, making a sudden decision, she drew in a slow, determined breath. "Therefore, I need to be going," she said, turning away from the two people whom she had come to love so dearly. Somehow, without her permission, Elsbeth had found a place in her heart, right alongside Allison. And Garrett...well, somehow he had managed to take away the ache left by Jeff and replace it with one of his own. Only his was going to hurt more.

Garrett reached out to stop her, but she quickly moved away from him. "Stay with us, Whitney," he whispered, his voice sounding as smooth as good whiskey.

"I...can't."

"Why do you keep running away?"

For just a moment she halted her retreat and squeezed her eyes shut to stop the tears. "Because I've got this feeling inside that tells me if I don't run away from you right now, then one day real soon you're going to take Elsbeth and walk away from *me*." Then, without glancing in his direction, she added, "Tell me I'm wrong, Garrett."

She felt his eyes boring into her back, but he remained silent. Finally, after what seemed like an eternity, he sighed heavily and said, "I can't lie to you. I'm sorry."

Whitney took a deep breath. "Yeah. So am I." Then she rushed from his house, only to cry herself to sleep in her own bed minutes later.

During the following days, Garrett and Whitney avoided having any physical contact with each other. Only when one of them had to pass Elsbeth to the other did their hands ever brush together. In the meantime

Whitney and Elsbeth fell into an easy routine that ended at the same time each afternoon when Garrett arrived home from work. Mrs. Ortego finally called to say she would be staying in Arkansas indefinitely. Whitney agreed to continue caring for Elsbeth until the woman returned. She tried convincing herself that she didn't have a choice, but in all honesty she knew she really didn't want one.

Now that Elsbeth was getting better from the chicken pox, she slept more peacefully and didn't require Whitney's full attention during nap time. To occupy those hours, Whitney found herself watering the vegetable garden outside, as well as doing Garrett and Elsbeth's laundry. She especially enjoyed ironing out the ruffles on some of Elsbeth's outfits and coordinating shorts and shirts and socks that later would make it easier on Garrett when he dressed Elsbeth.

On Monday of the following week Whitney suggested that Elsbeth was now well enough to be brought over to her house during the hours that she cared for her. In the past few days Garrett had become extremely quiet and thoughtful, almost disturbingly so. Apparently, Whitney decided, the grizzly in him was hibernating.

But on Friday afternoon of that week she was mildly surprised when she happened to glance at her wristwatch and realized that it was past time for Garrett to pick up Elsbeth.

Still, she wasn't terribly alarmed. But when an hour passed and he still hadn't arrived home, her worry began to mount.

Her first thoughts were that he'd had an accident, either on the job or on his way home. Then she convinced herself that her imagination was in maximum overdrive—it was probably only the afternoon rush-hour traffic that had him running late.

But when seven o'clock came around and he still hadn't returned, her dam of self-control sprang a major leak. She felt certain that something was wrong. Terribly wrong—or he would have been home by now. Or he would have called. Or sent someone to give her a message.

Or he would have done *something* to let her know what was going on.

Oh, God. What should she do? Whitney wondered, pacing the floor of her living room. She felt sick to her stomach. She went into the bedroom to check on Elsbeth and found her still asleep. Then, suddenly feeling as though she *had* to do something or go stark raving mad with worry, she hurried to the telephone and dialed the number at the construction site where Garrett worked. But just as she'd expected, no one answered. Next she dialed the company's main office and spoke to someone at the answering service, who said she didn't have any of the information that Whitney sought, and in an almost mechanical-sounding monotone, took Whitney's number and promised to have someone return her call.

At seven-thirty Whitney gave in to her ever-mounting fear and decided to phone the local hospital to ask if an accident victim with Garrett's name and description had been brought in. Maybe he was unconscious and couldn't telephone her. After several long, miserable minutes of waiting for the emergency operator to answer, she was finally told that no one with that name or description had been admitted into the hospital within the past eight hours. For some reason, though, Whitney wasn't quite convinced that the hospital employee had done as thorough a job of searching for information on Garrett as he claimed he had. Why didn't the man realize how important Garrett was to her and Elsbeth?

But in all honesty, she knew she was probably overreacting. Undoubtedly the emergency operator had done the best he could. Boy, if all her friends who thought she was always so cool and levelheaded in a crisis could see her now.

Calling the police was the only alternative she had left.

Just as she lifted the receiver to dial them, she heard a noise at the back of her house. Startled, she whirled around and accidently knocked over the small ceramic lamp on the desk right behind her. It crashed to the floor and broke into several large pieces. But at that moment the lamp was the least of Whitney's concerns; she was watching in horror as the knob on the back door first twisted one way and then the other.

Someone was trying to enter her house.

She sucked in a fright-filled breath and then fought back the scream that wanted to explode from her lungs. Dear God, if ever there was a time in her life to be levelheaded and calm, it was now.

A knock sounded lightly. "Whitney? Whitney, it's Garrett. Are you there?" he asked in a husky whisper. "Whitney, unlock the door and let me in."

Garrett? Did he say Garrett?

Yes, it was Garrett. She recognized his voice.

Relief washed over her, and she began to tremble. Fumbling for several moments, she finally managed to pull the door open. She immediately flung herself into Garrett's arms. "Oh, God, I thought something had happened to you."

"I'm all right," he reassured her, holding her around the waist with both arms. Whitney wanted to think that it was because he didn't want to ever let her go.

Which was just fine with her, because she knew one thing without a doubt. In his arms was where she belonged.

"Where's Elsbeth?" he asked.

"Sleeping in my room."

He gently pushed her toward the bedroom. "Bring her in here with us," he said breathlessly, wiping perspiration from his forehead.

"What? But she's sleeping."

"Whitney, just do as I say." This time his voice sounded rough. "And hurry it up."

Startled by his abrupt manner, Whitney tucked away her hurt feelings and rushed into the bedroom. Lifting the sleeping child into her arms, she held the little girl against her pounding heart.

She didn't truly understand why, but she felt her world was being threatened.

She walked back into the living room in time to see Garrett lowering the miniblind in her front window so that no one could see inside her house.

"What's going on, Garrett?" Her voice shook as she spoke.

Without glancing in her direction, he said, "I'll explain later. Right now I need to make sure I wasn't followed."

"Followed?" Whitney echoed in bewilderment.

"Did anyone come here today, asking questions about me?"

"Samantha came by at noon, but she didn't ask about you. Why?"

He shook his head. "Besides her."

"No...well—yes. There was a man—"

"A man?" Garrett cut in, hurrying to her. "Here?"

"Yes."

"When?"

"This morning. Around ten o'clock."

"What did he want?"

"He said he worked for the cable company and that they were checking out some problems they were having in the area. I told him I wasn't having any problems, and he left."

"Damn," Garrett replied, looking down at the floor as he cursed. "Did you happen to notice what he was driving?"

Fear gripped a tight band around Whitney's stomach, and she automatically hugged Elsbeth even closer. "No. Why?"

"Because I think he's found us."

Vats full of adrenaline were now being pumped into Whitney's body. "Who's found us? And what do they want?"

He was walking to another window and lowering the blinds. "The detective my ex-in-laws have hired to chase me down. And what he wants is Elsbeth."

"Elsbeth? Good God, did you steal her away from them?"

"No, of course not," he said, running frustrated fingers through his hair. "I won legal custody of her, just like I told you. Greta has visiting rights." He sighed heavily and looked out again between the slats of the miniblind.

"Look, my ex-in-laws were exercising Greta's visitation rights as their own. That in itself wasn't so bad, but then they began keeping her beyond the time we'd agreed upon. First they were an hour late. Then two hours. So

I put a stop to that. I just never realized how desperate they would become to have her under their complete control. Then it happened," he said, pausing to look out the window yet again.

"Garrett, for goodness' sakes, what happened?" Whitney exclaimed. "What did they do that was so terrible?"

"They tried to kidnap Elsbeth from me, that's what." Whitney looked stunned.

"Yeah," he said. "Shocking, isn't it? But it happens all the time. And it would have happened to Elsbeth if I hadn't arrived in time."

"Are you sure?" Whitney said.

He took a deep breath and them slumped down into a chair. "One Sunday afternoon I happened to be in the area where my ex-in-laws lived and decided to pick up Elsbeth from her visit with them instead of having them drive all the way to my place. Anyway, when I arrived, Greta's parents were outside and they were getting ready to place Elsbeth in a car with two complete strangers—people I'd never seen before."

"My God," Whitney replied. "What did you do?"

"I panicked, that's what I did. I could only see the car driving away with Elsbeth inside."

Whitney could tell by his facial expressions, as well as the tension in his body, that just talking about that afternoon was deeply difficult for him.

"Anyway," he continued, "it took me a moment to truly realize what was happening. Once I did, I started running toward the car. By this time I could see someone reaching out from the front seat to get Elsbeth from my ex-father-in-law's arms. I yelled out, and it must have startled them. Greta's father pulled Elsbeth back against him, and a second later the car sped off. I can still hear the sound of the tires squealing as they turned onto the main road."

"What did you do?"

"Nothing. There was nothing I could do. I didn't have an ounce of evidence. Oh, I accused them of trying to have Elsbeth kidnapped from me, but they denied everything. That's when I realized how truly dangerous they were."

"So you took Elsbeth and fled."

Garrett frowned. "Not that day. But after I got to thinking about what could have happened, I decided I didn't have much choice. Not immediately, anyway. I was afraid I'd get careless again, that next time they'd succeed in duping me."

Whitney fought the rising hurt as tears stung the corners of her eyes. "Did I ever tell you that my brother-in-law took my niece and just dropped out of sight in much the same way as you did with Elsbeth?" Her voice was shaking. "I loved her and I cared for her, but in the end it wasn't good enough. He still had the right to take her away, and there was nothing I could do."

"Whitney," Garrett said, reaching for her. "I didn't know—"

Suddenly, with Elsbeth still in her arms, Whitney turned and ran into her bedroom, slamming the door behind her. Elsbeth began to cry.

Garrett followed right behind her, but he was a second too late. Whitney locked the door just as he put his hand on the knob. "Whitney, let me in. We need to talk." He waited for her to do as he asked, but she didn't. Hands planted firmly on his hips, Garrett cursed himself for being a thoughtless bastard. He had ignored his own warnings about getting Whitney involved in his life. Like a starving man, he had been too hungry for too long to resist the warmth and compassion Whitney had offered him. And now she was suffering because of it.

If only he'd more time to explain things to her, to beg her forgiveness for taking such selfish advantage of her.

But time was a rare commodity for him these days, and all the wishful thinking in the world wasn't going to change that. His brother had called again last night and had told him that Greta was indeed in an exclusive rehabilitation clinic somewhere in Europe. The problem was that, in the meanwhile, her parents were trying to petition the courts—or as David had said, "pay off a judge," in order to gain custody of Elsbeth. Therefore, both his brother and his attorney thought it best if he and Elsbeth returned to San Francisco immediately.

And he knew they were right.

Life on the run was no kind of life for him and Elsbeth. Their only chance of ever obtaining normalcy again was for him to come face-to-face with his ex-in-laws and pray that the outcome of the battle that undoubtedly was going to take place would be in Elsbeth's best interest. If need be, he'd fight them all the way to the Supreme Court.

Which could take years. And most of his time and energy. And money.

He couldn't ask Whitney to wait for him indefinitely. Nor could he ask her to become involved in his battle. It wouldn't be fair. She'd already had enough pain in her life as it was. Leaving her now would be sheer hell, but it would spare her additional suffering on his account.

What a nightmare of a day, Garrett thought. First it had been the white four-door sedan that kept passing by the construction site, convincing him by late afternoon that it was indeed one of his ex-in-laws' thugs behind the wheel. Next had come the two-hour cat-and-mouse game he'd played after leaving work in order to lose the unwelcome tail. Then there had been the three-mile jog to Whitney's house because he didn't want to take any chances driving all the way home. And now this.

But one thing was painfully clear. He had come too far in his battle to keep Elsbeth safe to allow some hired thug to get the better of him. Come hell or high water, his daughter was going back to San Francisco the same way she'd left it. With him.

Only that meant leaving Whitney behind, and the mere thought hurt like hell.

As she sat on her bed cradling Elsbeth to her body, Whitney knew that she hadn't meant what she'd implied to Garrett. He was nothing like her brother-in-law. And the circumstances that had made him take his daughter away from her family were totally different from Jeff's.

She'd had no right to imply otherwise. Wouldn't she have done the same thing if Elsbeth had been hers?

Still, it didn't change anything. Garrett was still going to leave her, just as Jeff had done. Just as her father had done whenever he'd gone on a drinking binge. But maybe her father had been right about one thing; maybe she was too ordinary a person for any man, especially a man like Garrett, to love her enough to want her at his side forever.

No, she argued to herself, her spine stiffening. She was worthy of having a good man's love and she wasn't going to allow the insecurities of her past to undermine her confidence. She'd worked too hard in the past years to build up her self-esteem.

That was why she couldn't settle for less than what she wanted. And what she wanted was for Garrett to need her as much as she needed him. And if he didn't, then she couldn't let him know her true feelings for him. She just couldn't.

She stayed in her room with Elsbeth a little longer, sorting through the past weeks, allowing herself time to regain control over her emotions. She played peekaboo with Elsbeth for a while, then cried, finally realizing that she would have to hide away her feelings for Garrett and Elsbeth in order to be able to get on with her own life. The ache in her chest, however, didn't lessen just because she knew what she had to do.

Some of her friends were always telling her that life itself was a journey. If so, she couldn't help but wonder why she had chosen to travel it by means of a twisting, turning, narrow dirt road. An interstate would have been a lot smarter—and a whole lot safer for her emotions.

At some point Whitney stepped from the bedroom and realized immediately that Garrett was planning to leave her now. Two small duffel bags were placed near the front door. Her eyes rested on them for several seconds and then traveled to Garrett's face. He'd been patiently waiting for her to come out, but it was clear why. It was time to say goodbye.

"They're mine and Elsbeth's," he said without prevarication. "We're going back to San Francisco, first thing in the morning. Our flight leaves at six-forty. It's the only way I can get my life back together and give Elsbeth a normal upbringing. I know it's sudden, but..."

"I see," she replied, her whole body feeling as though it were going to explode into a million pieces. So she could easily be dispensed with. She was pleased when her voice came out fairly even, no trace of her raging grief at all. "Well, I'm glad to know you won't be needing my services any longer. I was beginning to get behind on my accounts.''

He started walking toward her. ''I know that Elsbeth and I became a burden to you. I've written you a check for your services,'' he said. ''It's on the kitchen table.''

Now that hurt.

''Thank you. But I can't accept it. I helped you out because it was the neighborly thing to do. You don't owe me anything.''

''I insist,'' he replied. ''It was always my intention to repay you for your kindness.''

By leaving me with a broken heart? Whitney screamed inside.

''Then I accept,'' she said, knowing full well she would never cash that check. Accepting, however, seemed the simplest way to end the conversation. ''Elsbeth's asleep. Should I wake her up to go home?'' It took every ounce of willpower she had not to burst into tears.

''I...well, I was hoping that we—Elsbeth and I— could stay here tonight. I haven't any reason to return to the house across the street, and I'd rather be here—uh— just in case the detective's found out my address. Besides, I'll have to ask you for one last favor.''

Whitney frowned. ''What's that?''

''Can you drive us to the airport? I left my Jeep at the shopping center three miles away when I spotted the tail. I didn't want to make it any easier for him to follow me here.''

The airport. God, did he know what he was asking of her? ''Why, of course.''

Whitney went into her bedroom and brought back a pillow and blanket for Garrett. ''I hope you'll be comfortable on the sofa.''

"I'll make do."

She turned to leave.

"Whitney?"

She faced him.

"Good night."

"Good night." Then she went to bed alone.

And Garrett stretched out on the sofa and stared up at the ceiling for the remainder of the night.

As a rule, Whitney didn't like airports. They were big and noisy and usually bustling with activity, and they always made her feel lonely. It seemed to her that someone was always leaving, and someone was always staying behind in them. They reminded her too much of her own life.

Garrett carried the duffel bags to the check-in counter, and Whitney carried Elsbeth. Then, all too soon, it was time to give her up. For a moment Whitney didn't think she would have enough willpower to do so. God help her, but she wanted to turn and run away with the little girl.

And she wanted Garrett to follow.

And she wanted them to live happily ever after in the Land of Enchantment.

But she knew better. This was the real world. There were no enchanted gardens, only glassed walls and huge metal jets waiting to be boarded. And no amount of wishful thinking on her part was going to change that.

Plain and simple, Garrett and Elsbeth were leaving her.

She would survive. Somehow. One day at a time. Piece by piece, she would pick up the fragments of her heart and paste them back together again. And one day she would be like new again.

Which was nothing more than wishful thinking on her part, and she knew it.

"Thanks for everything, Whitney," Garrett was saying. She looked up, and he was gazing at her with the saddest expression on his face. "I don't know if this is the neighborly thing to do or not, but—"

He leaned forward and placed the sweetest, the gentlest kiss on her mouth.

But then he was pulling away and hurrying down the corridor, with Elsbeth smiling and waving at Whitney from above her father's shoulder. Hot moisture stung Whitney's eyes as she blew tear-dampened kisses in their direction. Garrett didn't look back, but she waved goodbye to him, anyway, as well as to Elsbeth, until she could no longer see either of them in the crowd. Then, drained of all emotion, she dropped her hands to her sides and headed for home.

Upon landing in San Francisco, Garrett gathered up Elsbeth in his arms and prepared to disembark from the aircraft. Whitney was now hundreds of miles away, and every inch of distance between them had only added more pain to the ache in his heart.

He'd been a fool. A complete fool. He should have told her how he felt and let her make up her own mind as to whether or not she was willing to get mixed up in his life. Why hadn't he realized that hours ago? Days ago? The moment he'd known he was in love with her? Instead, he'd convinced himself to play the part of martyr. In the end he'd only made everyone—including himself—miserable. He needed Whitney. Elsbeth needed Whitney. And Whitney needed them. Their parting scene at the airport in Baton Rouge had been proof of that. He'd seen the sadness in her eyes. But like an idiot, he'd turned away, convincing himself that his main purpose right then was Elsbeth.

Well, his main purpose was still Elsbeth. But did that mean he didn't have needs, too? Wouldn't he fight a better fight on Elsbeth's behalf if he had the woman he loved at his side, loving him back and giving him the moral support he needed? The answer was crystal clear, and suddenly he knew what he had to do. But the big question was, when he went back, would Whitney forgive him for hurting her?

David was waiting for him at the airport, and by the time they arrived at their downtown office, he'd filled Garrett in on the latest happenings. It seemed that Greta was already back in town, sober and not very pleased with her parents. According to her lawyer, who had contacted Garrett's attorney, she wanted to make certain that her parents *didn't* get custody of Elsbeth—under any circumstances. Targeting them as the source of most of her emotional problems, she said she would go public with her accusations if they continued to give Garrett trouble where Elsbeth was concerned. Still wanting Garrett to have sole custody, she only requested that one day, when she got her life all together, she would be allowed to become a small part of her daughter's life again.

Garrett was elated with the news. No longer fearing the threat of an on-going court battle against his ex-in-laws, he felt free for the first time in months. Pleased to know that Greta was getting her life together, he used David's phone to contact his attorney. Garrett was more than willing to work with Greta on visitation rights whenever she felt she was ready.

And now *he* was ready to get on with his own life. Impatiently tying all of the loose ends he could for now, he quickly made sure everyone knew where he could be reached. Finally, assured that his attorney could handle the remaining details, he and Elsbeth boarded a jet that would take them back to Louisiana.

And once there, he was going to get down on his knees and beg Whitney to forgive him for leaving her behind. This time he wasn't going to be a fool. This time he was going to make her a promise he knew she needed to hear most of all. He was going to tell her that he would never leave her again. Not ever.

It had been four days since Garrett and Elsbeth had gone away. Four miserable days of trying to keep her thoughts focused on what she was doing, instead of what she was feeling. But it was impossible. At times the anguish was almost unbearable. Sometimes she found herself crying and she couldn't figure out whose memory had brought forth the renewed tears. Was it Lisa this time? Or Allison? Or was it from her latest heartaches, Garrett and Elsbeth? Then at some point she realized that she was grieving for all of them.

Samantha and her mother were worried sick about her. Sam made it a point to drop by at least twice a day, sometimes three, if she came home at noon for lunch. Whitney always assured them that she was fine, but somehow no one was buying it any more than she was.

Since the beginning of the week, she had designated this morning as housekeeping time. She'd just finished cleaning the kitchen and was dusting the furniture in her living room when she heard a knock at her door. Thinking it was undoubtedly Samantha, she shook her head in mild disbelief.

It wasn't that she didn't appreciate her friends and family being concerned about her, but enough was enough. And if Samantha continued to come home from work just to see about her like this, the company she worked for was going to make her start to use her sick leave.

Whitney pulled open the door with the intention of giving her best friend a good tongue-lashing for being such a worrywart; after all, she wasn't a child who needed constant attention. But instead of giving anyone a piece of her mind, she found herself shocked into silence as she stared at Garrett's handsome face. Then her eyes dropped to Elsbeth.

"Mum-mum," Elsbeth chimed, straddling her father's left hip. She rocked her small body back and forth. "Mum-mum."

"I think she's addressing you," Garrett said without making a move, the smoldering, intense look in his green eyes raising her temperature a degree or two.

Whitney's heart skipped a beat. "Oh, sweetheart," she exclaimed, taking Elsbeth from her father. "I missed you so."

Clearing his throat, Garrett looked down at his feet and then back up at Whitney. "She missed you, too. And so did I. But I'd understand if you told me to just take my kid and hit the road. I've been such a fool."

Whitney looked soulfully into his eyes. "Have you? Funny, but that's what I've been thinking about myself."

"You're not a fool," he said, his voice sounding choked up with emotion. "You're a warm, loving woman."

Whitney's smile was bittersweet. "I'm beginning to think that's a curse," she said.

"Someone from your past took unfair advantage of your kindness, didn't they?" Without glancing at him, and ignoring his last comment—yes, she'd been hurt, but that was in the past now—Whitney stepped back, and he entered the house. Then ever so gently, he reached out and began trailing his fingertips down the side of her face.

"Whitney, I'm sorry that I hurt you. I made a big mistake when I told you I had no choice but to leave you behind. I did need you with me. My only excuse is that at the time I thought I was doing the right thing. I didn't want you to get hurt by involving you in my problems." He shook his head. "I was too blind to see that I'd already done that by asking you to baby-sit Elsbeth. But if you'll give me another chance, if you'll let me explain everything . . . then I—I promise you I won't make that mistake again. And I'll never leave you. In fact, I couldn't even if I wanted to. I love you too much to live without you."

"Da-da," Elsbeth said, reaching up and patting Garrett on the face with her chubby little hand. "Mum-mum," she said, doing the same to Whitney. Then, clapping her hands together, she sang, "Patty-cake, patty-cake."

Whitney and Garrett smiled into each other's eyes.

Through tears of joy, Whitney said, "I think she's just made us into a family."

Garrett shook his head. "No, Whitney. You're the one who's made us into a family. You're one heck of a woman."

And then he was kissing her and whispering words of endearing love.

And that was when Whitney knew for certain that her father had been wrong all along. She had never been ordinary. For surely the gift of love that this man was offering her was fit for any queen.

Whitney recalled the Saturday morning when she and Garrett had spoken to each other for the first time in the supermarket parking lot. The day his shopping bag had burst and she had helped him gather up his scattered groceries. At the time she'd thought him to be an old grizzly.

But now, after all that had happened between them, she couldn't help but wonder how someone with her fair amount of intelligence could have been so utterly mistaken.

"I love you, Garrett. For always and always."

"Then prove it," he growled, pulling her closer and deepening the kiss. Against her mouth, he added in a husky voice, "As soon as Elsbeth is asleep."

Whitney's stomach quivered at the thought. And much to her surprise, she found herself overwhelmingly pleased to discover that the wild animal in him had not been tamed at all.

Once a grizzly, always a grizzly.

Smiling at her beloved, she said, "Then take me to your hideaway and we can hibernate together."

His laughter was deep and rich as it echoed through her house. He entangled his fingers in her hair and placed his warm mouth against her ear. "Your every wish is my command."

Even though she still had one heartache, Whitney felt she would burst with everlasting happiness as she found herself being healed from the hurts of the past by the steady hand of Garrett and Elsbeth's love.

And then, from somewhere deep inside her soul, she somehow knew that, someday, her heart would be completely mended.

Someday she would see Allison again.

*   *   *   *   *

**Three All-American beauties discover
love comes in all shapes and sizes!**

ALL-AMERICAN SWEETHEARTS

by Laurie Paige

CARA'S BELOVED (#917)—*February*
SALLY'S BEAU (#923)—*March*
VICTORIA'S CONQUEST (#933)—*April*

A lost love, a new love and a hidden one, three *All-American Sweethearts* get their men in Paradise Falls, West Virginia. Only in America . . . and only from Silhouette Romance!

Silhouette
R O M A N C E™

A romantic collection that
will touch your heart....

to Mother with Love '93

Diana Palmer
Debbie Macomber
Judith Duncan

As part of your annual tribute to
motherhood, join three of Silhouette's
best-loved authors as they celebrate the
joy of one of our most precious gifts—
mothers.

Available in May at your favorite retail outlet.

Only from 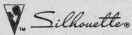 *Silhouette*®

—where passion lives.